TOWN TAMER

Stepping down from the stagecoach in the heat of mid-morning, he was a medium-tall man with the thin flanks of a horseman and the flat gray stare of a gunfighter; his name was Ethan Scott. But no one needed to ask his name. They knew him without asking. A sweeping black mustache guarded his wide lips and his deepset eyes were shadowed by black brows. His jaw had a slight jut to it and his hair, when he swept off his hat to wipe his forehead with a kerchief, was raven black atop his high brow.

He would have been handsome except for his eyes. They were cold and impersonal and deadly as a snake's.

He moved slowly, with a predator's suppleness and smoothness; he did not glare and he did not boast, and he threatened no one, except with the bleakness of his hollow gray eyes; yet he was, they said, the toughest man in Arizona.

Also by Brian Garfield, available from Bantam Books

THE PALADIN
THE THOUSAND-MILE WAR
APACHE CANYON
THE ARIZONAN

VULTURES IN THE SUN

BRIAN GARFIELD

BANTAM BOOKS
TORONTO · NEW YORK · LONDON · SYDNEY · AUCKLAND

VULTURES IN THE SUN

A Bantam Book / published by arrangement with the author
Bantam edition / May 1987

ISBN 0-553-26331-5

Published simultaneously in the United States and Canada

Bantam Books are published by Bantam Books, Inc. Its trademark, consisting of the words "Bantam Books" and the por-
trayal of a rooster, is Registered in U.S. Patent and Trademark
Office and in other countries. Marca Registrada. Bantam
Books, Inc., 666 Fifth Avenue, New York, New York 10103.

PRINTED IN THE UNITED STATES OF AMERICA

O   0 9 8 7 6 5 4 3 2 1

VULTURES
IN THE SUN

I

A LONG TIME AGO, in his youth, he had been a horseman with all the skill of expert habit; now he was only a grossly fat man slouched uncomfortably in the swaying saddle. His name was Eugenio Castillo, and it happened that he was the duly elected sheriff of Mescalero County, down in the central-eastern district of Arizona Territory.

The sheriff's thighs were as thick as a cowboy's waist; his hands were massive. His eyes were noncommittal, his expression uncertain; and he wore a weighty black mustache that drooped by the corners of his mouth. The brim of his floppy hat shaded his brown complexion.

Bit chains jingled at his bay horse's jaws. The sun slapped his shoulders violently. And now, three miles out of Lodestar on the coach road, he reined in the jogging pony and sat frowning at the ground through the thin turbulence of risen dust. The horse fidgeted and he reined it under control; he swung his right leg over the horse's rump and stepped stiffly to the ground, grunting. Leaving the split reins to trail, he walked forward, staring through half-shuttered lids at the dusty road advancing under his feet.

Once he paused, crouching down with effort to examine the earth more closely. A murmur escaped his lips: "Right here. It was right here it happened." His tones were very lightly liquid with Spanish intonations.

He stood up, still frowning, and waddled as far as a scraggly mesquite bush by the road's edge, where he again hunkered down, thinking. His glance flicked up to the horizon close by, where the southward tack of the coach road disappeared over a hill on its way to Lodestar, and he sat motionless, arrested by sight of a thickening plume of

1

dust rising just beyond that hilltop. In time the approaching disturbance rose to view and became a single trotting horse towing a light buggy. Shadows thrown by the buggy's top obscured the driver, but Sheriff Castillo did not need to see the face. The buggy was instantly recognizable: it belonged to Guy Murvain. For that matter, there were a good many articles in this corner of the country that belonged to Guy Murvain. Murvain owned the Hilltop Mine, the Hilltop Smelter, the Hilltop Freight Company, and several other properties in and around Lodestar.

The horse advanced at a steady gait, pulling the buggy bouncing behind it, and Sheriff Castillo stood up once more, making his corpulent way to the center of the coach road, where he stood heavily, frowning. His frown now was different from the frown before. Before he had been puzzled, questioning; now he was irritated. He had a pretty good idea of what was on Guy Murvain's mind. He could almost predict the words Murvain would use.

For no particular apparent reason, Murvain halted his buggy beside the sheriff's horse, climbed down from the buggy and walked across the fifty-foot distance between them. His suit of black broadcloth was coated with fine dust. "It happened here," Murvain said in his habitual arrogant baritone.

"Somehow," Sheriff Castillo said drily, "I could see that for myself."

Murvain let the sheriff's sarcasm ride over his shoulder; he ignored it. "Seems to be enough horse sign around here for a small army. How many did you say there were?"

"Your muleskinner told me there was maybe eight, maybe ten. He was a little rattled—I don't guess he stopped to count."

"It's of no account," Murvain said. "What matters is the payroll. They got my payroll, and shot my wagon guard."

"That they did," the sheriff said.

Murvain flushed. His expression narrowed across the block of his face and his voice turned resentful: "You know who stole that payroll and so do I, Gene. What do you intend to do about it?"

"Look for evidence," the sheriff replied mildly.

"Evidence!"

The sheriff nodded; his chins wobbled. "Evidence. Your wagon driver didn't recognize any of them."

"Hell," Murvain said sourly. "I didn't even see them and I can recognize them. It was Henry Dierkes and some of his toughs."

"Maybe," Castillo said, and Murvain, thickset and square-jawed, did not reply. Murvain only stood his ground and kept his thinly screened glare on the sheriff. Castillo met his glance without malice. "Go on home."

"What?"

"You're in my way," the sheriff said, and started to turn away.

Murvain's powerful arm shot forward, arresting him; Murvain's eyes gleamed with indignant anger and he said, "Wait just a minute, Gene. There was a lot of money on that wagon today, all of it mine."

"None of it yours," Castillo replied. "It belonged to the miners that work for you. Didn't it?"

Murvain clamped his jaws. "Don't quibble. Damn it, for all we know, Henry Dierkes is within a quarter of a mile of here, watching us and laughing his head off."

"What if he is?"

"Jesus," Murvain muttered. "You Mexicans are all alike. I'll be damned if I've ever got a straight answer out of you yet, Gene."

Castillo smiled gently. "You always expect the wrong answer. Don't blame me for that."

"Aagh," Murvain said in disgust. He cuffed his hat back and glared at the surrounding desert hills. "Gene, in the past five years this county has become hideout and headquarters for damn near every tough in the Southwest. It's supposed to be your job to get rid of them. You haven't. I think it's about time we tried on a new sheriff for size."

"Suit yourself."

"Maybe I'll do just that!"

"Just remember one thing," the sheriff said quietly. "Any sheriff you get will be bound by the letter of the law, just like me. I can't arrest a man without proof he's committed a crime. I can't run a man out just on the say-so of you or some other wealthy gent. Neither could any other lawman you hired."

Murvain's tone turned soft and flat. "Do you know how much was on that wagon they held up today? Eighteen thousand dollars. Two months' payroll—because Henry Dierkes and his cutthroats held up last month's payroll shipment too. That means I'll have to bring in another payroll to pay off my men at Hilltop. It means if you don't bring in Dierkes and his men pretty damn fast, I'll lose my insurance—and my insurance doesn't cover the whole of a big loss anyway. It means the Hilltop mine can go broke. And if I go broke and a few other mines go under, your whole damned town will fold up and die. Is that what you want?"

"No," Castillo said.

"Then maybe what you want is for the federal government to declare that this is an area of martial law, the way they did with Tombstone a few years ago. Maybe we ought to bring in the Earp boys and have another bloodbath like they had at Tombstone too. Hey?"

"Simmer down," the sheriff told him.

"Simmer down, hell!" But then Murvain's forehead ridged and his mouth pursed, and he said in a lower voice, "Wait a minute—maybe I had something there."

"What?"

"What I just said about the Earps."

Castillo just looked at him over a stretching interval. Then he threw back his fat face and broke into loud laughter. Murvain's thick-fingered hand shot forward and cuffed his cheek, and Castillo subsided. Murvain said, "You think it's funny?"

The sheriff felt the sting in his cheek; he let himself cool down before he answered. "The Earps were run out of Arizona, old friend. You couldn't get them back here on a bet. And if you did, you wouldn't be able to trust them any farther than you trust Henry Dierkes."

Murvain waved his hand in a gesture, dismissing it. "I didn't mean it that way. Not the Earps personally. But a gun. Suppose we hired a gun?"

"One gun? What good would one gun do? You're the one who was just talking about all the toughs up in the

Yellows. How many of them you figure there are? Sixty? Ninety? A hundred, maybe?"

"One gun's enough," Murvain said, "if it's a good enough gun. Who's the toughest man in Arizona, Gene? Doc Holiday?"

"He's in Colorado," the sheriff said.

"Who, then? Ike Clanton? Burt Alvrod? Ethan Scott?"

"Probably Ethan Scott," the sheriff conceded. "Ike Clanton talks tough, but he ain't. Burt Alvrod—you never know where he stands. Look, why don't you just hire Henry Dierkes? He's as tough as any of them."

"Don't try to be funny," Murvain said. "It doesn't fit you. But that's the answer, Gene. Dierkes may be tough, but not as tough as Ethan Scott."

"Maybe," Castillo said skeptically. "Dierkes likes to laugh, but when he wants a fight, I've yet to see the man could knock him down. He's strong and he's fast and he's shrewd, Henry Dierkes. I wouldn't want to bet Ethan Scott could whip him."

"I would," Murvain said softly. "That's the difference between you and me, Gene. It takes a man with backbone to make a bet like that."

The sheriff showed no offense. "There's some difference, I've seen, between a man with backbone and a stubborn fool."

Murvain smiled coolly. His face had settled into a self-certain mask. "What you don't seem to realize is that I've got my back to the wall. All of us do. If we can't find some way to stop Dierkes, we'll go under, all together in a heap. Listen to me, Sheriff—I don't aim to let that happen. If it takes fire to fight fire, then it takes an Ethan Scott to fight a Henry Dierkes. My mistake's been not seeing that sooner."

"Take it easy," Castillo said. "Think awhile before you go off half-cocked, my friend. I've seen Ethan Scotts come and I've seen 'em go, and I never saw a one of them that didn't leave a backtrail littered with grief."

Sunlight rippled in reflection on the dusty ground. Guy Murvain was shaking his blunt head back and forth; he said, "You don't get this yet, do you? You're a good politician, Gene, but what this district needs is a man with spine and a quick gun. Now I'll tell you what you do. You take your horse and follow these tracks here and see where they get you. I'll match any odds they'll just peter out in the traffic down the road. But while you're out here wasting time in the hills and looking for evidence that's not to be found, I'll be getting something done. Something I should have done a long time ago."

And with that, Murvain turned away perfunctorily, strode to his buggy and climbed up to the seat. Unruffled, the sheriff stood where he was, watching. Murvain kicked the brake off, lifted his reins and clucked to the horse; the light rig turned a small circle within the rims of the road and headed back for town, the pony trotting and the buggy bouncing.

Sheriff Castillo watched without expression until Murvain's buggy was absorbed by the distance. Then the fat sheriff lifted his pudgy hand and shrugged his shoulders, dropped his hand and went to his horse. His cross was the weight he carried; he used a lot of energy climbing into the saddle, and when it was done he sat breathing heavily, wiping sweat from his face with the back of his hand.

Finally he put the horse north along the road and let the rising slope carry him along to the top, where he hesitated long enough to look back from this position of command and see the diminishing dust spire of Guy Murvain's buggy. Then the sheriff went down the far side of the hill, glancing now and then at the prolific tracks extending before him. The road undulated northward, making a slight loop around a cliff protruberence, which was an irregular jutting portion of the Mogul Rim. The Mogul Rim ran from a point well south of Lodestar, in a more or less northerly direction, until it came past the town of Spanish Flat, which lay thirty miles north. Then the Rim cut back, pushing the Yellows with it, and finally dropped off to an end. But all along its course it formed a high escarpment definitely marking the edge of the deep, high range of mountains that were the Yellows. Here and there were eroded notches vee-ing down, slicing the rim, giving access to the higher mountain reaches to the east;

and that country yonder, the summit passes of the Yellows, was Henry Dierkes's country.

Sheriff Castillo thought of all the things he knew, and presently his lips moved slowly: "Nothing Guy Murvain can say or do will ever change the face of this country."

Having made this sage observation, the sheriff let the road lift him past one more hilltop before he halted in the shade of a cottonwood that spread beside a dry creek. He was that way, bending his head to light up a cigar, when hoofbeats telegraphed along the creekbed gravel, clattering; and the sheriff's hatbrim rose sharply.

The oncoming horseman was a tall young man with lean hips and black hair; he was hatless and clean-shaven, thereby violating the custom of the country, and his costume, by the grace of its cut and the finery of its cloth, made plain that the rider was a man of some wealth, young as he seemed. He wore a split-tail frock coat even in this heat; and that was what made Sheriff Castillo shake his head with wonder. That rider, the one advancing without hurry, was Tom Larrabee, who owned the Lodgepole Mining Company, second in size only to Murvain's Hilltop. The sheriff did not fail to mark the coincidence that would have him meet the county's two wealthiest men on a lonely road in such quick succession; but it was another consideration that pushed aside such idle speculation: Larrabee's coat. Larrabee wore one frock coat or another at all times, winter or summer, day or night. It was a sign of the man's unbending will, a sign that Tom Larrabee would never step back from anyone or anything. The frock coat was merely an obvious, and an intentional, symbol proclaiming to the world that this man would no sooner admit another man's greater strength that he would admit the greater strength of the elements.

Larrabee, now within a few hundred yards, was coming forward from the east, from the Mogul Rim, from the direction of the Yellows—and this was another source of wonder to the sheriff. Larrabee's mine was far south of this parallel, and the sheriff could not offhand imagine any errand that would put Larrabee in this particular region, so close to the edges of the territory that Henry Dierkes claimed to control with his rawhiders. It could be a strange breed of range politics, the sheriff reflected; on the other hand it might just be Larrabee's way of showing his scornful disregard for the power of the toughs.

Larrabee crossed the last hundred feet between them with a withdrawn, secret kind of smile playing around his lips; he hauled in his reins and halted his mount with more show and more savagery than was necessary, and waited for the horse to calm down and the dust to settle before he folded his hands together on the saddlehorn and said, "Good day, Sheriff."

"Buenos dias," Castillo murmured.

Tom Larrabee's smile fled; brief irritation replaced it. "Don't talk Mexican at me, Sheriff."

"Sure," Castillo said in the same imperturbable tone. "Want me to talk Papago? My old woman was a Papago."

Larrabee glared at him for a moment; then some other stray thought seemed to pass by, for Larrabee suddenly chose to ignore the sheriff's baiting. The young man's dark and handsome face relaxed back into its mocking smile and he said, "I don't suppose you'd be out this far if it was just a ride for your health, Sheriff. On business today?"

"I am."

"Something happen?"

"One of Guy Murvain's wagons was held up today."

"Think of that," Larrabee said. "The payroll?"

"Yes."

Larrabee shook his head; but the smile remained. "Guy can't afford too many more robberies. How much did he lose this time?"

"Too much," the sheriff said. "How much have you lost?"

"Too much," Larrabee echoed in reply.

"Tell me," the sheriff said, "where were you today?"

Larrabee flushed, but then shrugged, speaking idly. "Why not? You're entitled to know, I guess." He smiled again, as if with some secret knowledge that sparked his amusement, and went on with seemingly unconscious glibness: "A fellow offered to sell me his mining claim up above the Rim, back there. I went up just now to look at it."

"Just to look? Or maybe to throw a dare at Henry Dierkes?"

"Just to look," Larrabee said.

"And?"

"The claim's worthless. I didn't buy it, of course. If you want to check my story with him, I'll take you up there. Want to go?" Larrabee was almost boastful, as though he were sure the sheriff wouldn't accept an invitation to ride up toward Henry Dierkes's domain. The sheriff, however, had no reluctance to ride into Dierkes's country, and no particular reason, on the other hand, to call Larrabee's bluff; and so he said: "I've got no reason to disbelieve you. I'll let it pass."

"Good of you," Larrabee said, his voice as dry as the dust stirred by his roan's hoofs.

The sheriff ignored him. "You know," he mused, "Guy Murvain said a funny thing a little while ago."

"What was that?"

"He said he was thinking about sending for Ethan Scott."

"What?"

"That's what he said," the sheriff told him. "Now, it might be you could cool him down some. I don't know what this county needs for a cure, but there's one thing it don't need, and that's a hired gun. I've seen enough bloodshed in my time."

Larrabee tilted his hatless head slightly to the side. A light gust of air ruffled his black hair. "Are you tired of it, Sheriff, or just afraid?"

"Afraid of what?"

"I've known men," Larrabee murmured, "who were afraid every moment of their lives." A light of contempt and strong ambition shone briefly from his eyes; he dipped his head, lifted the reins and trotted away, heading down the coach road toward Lodestar.

Wearing a puzzled expression on his fat cheeks, Sheriff Castillo watched the young Pennsylvanian disappear; then he rode out of the shade, felt the sun strike his back, and cut overland in the general direction of the Mogul Rim. No longer did he bother keeping up the pretense of looking for tracks in the ground. Presently he encountered a grove of cottonwoods lining the banks of a mud-floored gully; he trotted up the floor of that trough and pulled up into the trees after carefully sweeping the horizons and finding no one in sight.

Then he did a strange thing: he dismounted, made his way into the deep shade of a thick cottonwood in the midst of the grove, and sat down on thin yellow grass by the bole of the tree. He stretched his fat legs before him, planted the width of his back against the tree, pulled up a grass stalk to chew on and pushed his hat forward over his face; he folded his arms, breathing a heavy sigh, and closed his eyes, relying on his perceptive ears to warn him if anyone drew near.

But he heard nothing more than the sound of his own breathing and the occasional breath of wind in the branches overhead. He spent the better part of the afternoon that way, in a dozing half-sleep, and after a while, when the sun came around the tree and began to warm up his flesh, he rose, stretched, and adjusted his hat before waddling downstream to his horse, which had wandered grazing. When he mounted he glanced at the sun's westward position in the sky—he had no timepiece of his own—and judged that he had spent enough time in the country. So deciding, he put his horse south-by-southwest, toward Lodestar and the comfort of his office.

II

HEAT AND POWDERY yellow dust lay close along the surface of the broad, bright street. Coming around the corner from Third into Bow Street, Krayle MacIver stopped on the boardwalk and grinned toward no one in particular. He was a short man, thin, and though he was only thirty-seven, his hair and mustache were silver-gray.

He stopped in the yard-wide splash of shadow along the corner's boardwalk and rammed his hands into his pockets, enjoying an easy morning's indolence. His Justin walking boots were polished to a high luster, though slightly filmed over by the morning's coat of dust; and by his dress—tailored gray suit and ruffled white shirt with string tie—it could be told easily enough that Krayle MacIver was a man of taste, and that he was a man of means. His hat was gray felt, flat-crowned and only slightly curled at the last half-inch of brim. He was a sharp-chinned man with wide, sensitive lips and a blade of a nose, beside which his long blue eyes were set evenly. Though his face was narrow and more delicate than most, it had a pleasing regularity.

A man came up along the Bow Street walk, moving with a self-important stride and quick lunges of his thick arms; that man was Guy Murvain, owner of the Hilltop enterprises, and when Murvain came by he dipped his head with cool but civil courtesy and said, "Morning, MacIver."

MacIver nodded and watched Murvain go on up the street. Pedestrian traffic was light on the boardwalks. MacIver stepped off the boardwalk and walked across Bow Street. He detoured around the back of a slow-moving freight wagon, drawn by eight teams of mules, and stepped up on the corner, pausing momentarily to look up at the big, brightly painted sign above the corner doorway: NUGGET SALOON AND PALACE OF CHANCE, the sign read; MacIver smiled and stepped inside.

It was a huge room, and he viewed it with pride, for this was all his—it belonged to Krayle MacIver. From the doorway he surveyed its dimensions: almost a hundred feet long and seventy wide, it held fifty tables, each surrounded by four chairs. The ceiling was fifteen feet high, supported by sculptured wooden columns at regular intervals. Twenty-four crystal chandeliers hung there, each one of them ornate and big enough to dominate a smaller room.

The floor on which he stood was polished hardwood; the bar, running two-thirds the length of one wall, was glistening dark walnut with a stout brass rail near the floor. Behind the bar hung six oblong mirrors; between the mirrors were shelves of bottles and glassware; and above the center mirror was hung the huge painting of Marla Searles. Whenever he entered the Nugget—and he did so several times daily—that portrait became the focal point of his attention. He had commissioned it several years ago, in St. Louis, and the artist had done justice to Marla. In all her supple perfection she lay along a couch, dressed in a flowing vermilion gown, smiling out of the canvas in the way only Marla could smile.

But she wasn't smiling. The painting smiled, but Marla didn't. She walked forward from the back of the room toward the bar, wearing a dark green divided riding skirt and a silk blouse. A riding crop was in her gloved hand and her mass of heavy auburn hair was tied back in a bun. She walked around the standing figures of half a dozen men scattered along the bar. Her expression was level, even, steady—and blank. When she wanted to, MacIver thought, Marla could conceal every thought and every feeling behind the forced blandness of her cheeks. MacIver grimaced slightly and waited while she came forward. She met him at the bar. Only a few customers were in the place; the two bartenders stood patiently and wearily. MacIver watched the girl's face for a break of expression. He found none. He said, "Going for a ride?"

"Yes."

"Be careful," he said. "You know the kind of men who ride those hills."

"I know them," she said. She smiled a wholly synthetic smile, the same brand of smile she used while she was on the Nugget's stage, singing. "I've handled men in here. I can handle them out in the hills, too, when I have to."

MacIver pointed toward the tiny revolver holstered at her waist. "That popgun won't do you much good."

"It's enough." Her voice was low in her throat; it's tone told him nothing. "The one thing I've learned to appreciate about the toughs is that they have one code. They don't trouble women."

"Don't be too sure," he said, and watched her swing away toward the door. Her hips rolled faintly, suggestively. Then her lean, graceful figure was out of sight and MacIver turned, putting his belly to the bar. "Give me a beer, Sandy."

The bartender nodded and held a clay mug under the spigot of a keg. By the time he had handed the tepid beer to MacIver, a newcomer had arrived at the bar—Price Lafayette, editor of the *Lodestar Daily Compass*. And since Lafayette was something of a leader of opinion in the community, MacIver accorded him the courtesy of nodding and signaling to the bartender: "Another beer, Sandy."

"Thank you," Price Lafayette drawled, and put his mildly amused and speculative eyes on MacIver. Lafayette was a tall and gangling fellow, almost entirely bald. His eyes were wide and round; his lips were quizzically set; and his Adam's apple bobbed continuously. He said, "I assume you've heard the latest news from the mine owners' combine."

MacIver sipped foam off his beer. "Which?"

"They've sent off for Ethan Scott."

MacIver nodded. "Guy Murvain's stupid idea, isn't it? But nothing will come of it."

"What makes you say that?"

"I'm well acquainted with Ethan Scott," MacIver said. He took a few short sips of beer and turned to lean his elbow against the bar, facing Lafayette. "He's a very old friend of mine. I don't think he'll want this job."

"Why shouldn't he?"

MacIver's shoulders lifted slightly and dropped. "Ethan Scott's no fool. He knows Henry Dierkes—and even if the odds don't stop him, one look at Guy Murvain will."

"What do you mean by that?"

MacIver smiled gently at the editor; Lafayette was pumping him—his reaction would undoubtedly appear in tomorrow's paper, for Krayle MacIver was a citizen of some importance in the city. "I don't think Ethan would want to work for Guy Murvain. I won't put it any plainer than that."

"Murvain wouldn't be hiring him," Lafayette said. "If Scott comes to Lodestar, it will be the combine that hires him—all the mine owners together."

MacIver shook his head. "That wouldn't fool Ethan Scott for ten seconds. Murvain *is* the combine for all practical purposes. He cracks the whip."

"No," Lafayette said. "He's not that powerful. Murvain

talks a bigger brand of power than he owns. But I admit I'm in agreement with him on one thing. This organized outlawry has got to stop. If it isn't under control, the mines will close—and Lodestar will die with them. None of us can afford to let that happen."

"And therefore you're in favor of hiring Ethan Scott. Is that it?"

"Yes."

MacIver looked at him with some surprise. "I always thought of you as a law-and-order man. What about the sheriff?"

"Castillo's a soft man," Lafayette said. "He tries, I suppose—but it's not enough. Certainly I'm a law-and-order man. I want to see law and order in this neck of the woods. Don't we all?"

"I'm not sure," MacIver murmured. "As a law-and-order advocate, you'd condone hiring Ethan Scott?"

"What other way have we of controlling Dierkes?" Lafayette flushed. MacIver watched him with quiet interest; and Lafayette said, "You say you're a friend of Ethan Scott's. And yet you seem to think there's something wrong with him—some reason we shouldn't hire him."

"I don't think you shouldn't hire him," MacIver said. "But if I had your views and your ethics, I'd hesitate."

"Why?"

MacIver stood silent a moment, composing his answer. A few men drifted into the big room, and one customer left; one of the bartenders stirred briefly, filled a few orders and relapsed to his quiet stand. MacIver considered the tall editor—Lafayette's bald head gleamed faintly—and presently said, "Do you remember Tombstone, Price?"

"Yes. What of it?"

"The toughs took Tombstone over. Then the law-and-order people decided to clean up the town. Wells, Fargo hired Wyatt Earp as a shotgun guard. The city hired gunfighters to enforce the laws—Billy Breakenridge and Fred White and Virgil Earp. And right away the trouble started. Fred White was killed, Morgan Earp was killed. The McLowery brothers and Billy Clanton, Ringo and Curly Bill—I think I could name you a dozen men, all of them dead because of the Earps and the Clantons. A lot of men were crippled, like Virgil Earp. There was vigilante law and necktie parties and wholesale butcherings down in Mexico, half of them led by Earp's friend Doc Holliday. Is that what you want here?"

"Ethan Scott isn't Wyatt Earp."

"They follow the same star," MacIver said softly.

Lafayette frowned over his beer. "Just what kind of man is he?"

Ethan Scott. MacIver thought back across the dusty years and after a while he said, "A quiet man. Bottled up tight—and full of explosive. He's withdrawn and polite and he's probably the toughest man in this country. Is that an answer? It's as good as I can give you."

"Is he honest? Is he loyal to his hire?"

"As much as anyone, I suppose. He's a great pacifier, I'll admit—but I'm not sure you people want the kind of peace he'll bring. Its cost is high."

"We'll pay him handsomely."

"That's not what I meant," MacIver breathed. "You miss my point."

Lafayette frowned; after a moment he said, "Are you recommending that we forget it?"

"I'm not recommending anything," MacIver replied smoothly.

"Well," Lafayette said in a slightly uncertain manner, "we're holding a council meeting this afternoon to talk it over. Will you be there?"

MacIver chuckled. "It wouldn't be much of a meeting without me, Price. I'll be there."

Lafayette nodded his tall, bald head and donned his bowler hat. He was half-turned toward the entrance when the crackle of gunfire erupted somewhere outside and Lafayette's hatrim snapped up. "What's that—what's that?"

"Probably some fool cowboy," MacIver guessed. The single ragged volley had ended and there was no more shooting. "Shooting up the town out of deviltry," MacIver finished; but just the same he was on his way to the door, to investigate. Close on his heels he felt the following presence of the editor.

MacIver went through the doorway at a half-run and

hesitated on the corner; then boots scuffed the dirt behind him, down Third Street to the east, and he wheeled that way, sending his quick glance hurling along the walk. What he saw was a small, quickly growing crowd of men standing around a prone body that was occasionally visible between shifting, milling legs. MacIver heard Price Lafayette's dry comment: "Somebody got in the way of the cowboy's fun, eh, MacIver?"

He didn't stop to answer; he stretched his short legs, striding across the half-block distance to the crowd. Lafayette stayed close behind. MacIver reached the edge of the crowd and used his small body as a wedge, driving forward to the inside of the circle.

He noticed then, for the first time, that another man was right beside him: Sheriff Eugenio Castillo. The sheriff's wide, corpulent shape squeezed past and crouched by the prone man. Another man crouched there too, a thick-shouldered man with a spare line of a mouth and the hat of a cowboy. MacIver stood by, listening; the sheriff said, "All right, Arnie."

Arnie was the cowboy crouched by the dead man. Arnie's voice was scratchy and reluctant: "You know him?"

The sheriff looked down at the dead man. "No."

"Miner name of Murphy," Arnie said. "Worked for Hilltop."

"And?"

"He prodded me into it," Arnie said.

Price Lafayette whispered to MacIver: "I'll bet he did." Lafayette had his notebook and pencil out.

"Go on," the sheriff told Arnie.

"He was a little drunk, Sheriff. He made a few remarks. I tried to let them pass, but then he accused me of holdin' up the payroll wagon yesterday."

Lafayette whispered again, "Did he, now?"

"And so you killed him," the sheriff said to Arnie.

"No. He took a shot at me as I was turnin' away. I'm just lucky he missed me, is all. Hell, Sheriff—there must be a few people around here who seen it. We wasn't alone on the street. Didn't any of you folks see him shoot at me?"

"I saw it," a man said, and stepped forward out of the

crowd. MacIver didn't recognize the man, but apparently the sheriff did. The witness said, "Look at Murphy's gun. He fired it twice."

The gun lay a few inches from the dead man's extended hand. The sheriff picked it up, sniffed the barrel, opened the frame-gate and turned the cylinder slowly to look at the primers of each cartridge. Then he nodded and stood up. "Looks plain enough, Arnie. Be available for the coroner's inquest, will you?"

"All right," Arnie said. He looked at the dead man's face. There was no regret in Arnie's expression. "Can I go now?"

"You can go."

Arnie stood up and put his back to them and went away through the crowd. The sheriff's voice reached MacIver dimly: "A couple of you take Murphy over to the coroner's."

It was just the repetition of an old game that he had seen many a time; but nonetheless MacIver's stomach tightened and he turned away. At his shoulder Price Lafayette said, "A fine example of justice, isn't it? What will you bet Murphy's accusation was right? Ten to one Arnie was one of the toughs who held up that payroll shipment on the coach road."

"I wouldn't know," MacIver said distantly. "I wasn't there."

"Well," Lafayette said, "I've got to write this up. I'll see you at the meeting this afternoon."

"Yes." MacIver's voice was an absent-minded murmur. Lafayette's long legs carried the editor away and after a while MacIver went down the walk to the corner and turned inside the Nugget. He took a drink at the bar and then restlessness prompted him outside again; he stood on the boardwalk beside the Nugget door, teetering on his heels, putting a hand inside his coat to draw a cheroot from his pocket. He lit the cheroot, broke his match and tossed it in the street. The crowd down Third Street was breaking up. A couple of men were carrying the body away. The sheriff's hat shape appeared and advanced; the sheriff went past MacIver without speaking and turned up Bow Street toward the courthouse. MacIver hooked his thumbs in the armholes of his brocade vest while he tilted his head back and observed, with morose interest, the sharply and all-too-obviously-drawn line of demarcation that the center of Bow Street represented. The far side of the street, the west side, and everything beyond it, was the respectable side of Lodestar. There the good citizens of Lodestar lived and worked and gathered. Above, two blocks to the north, the three-storied National Hotel dominated the street, and walking down from there a pedestrian would pass in front of the Overland office, the firehouse of Engine Company Number Two, the Wells, Fargo office, and then, after the intersection of Second, the Mescalero County courthouse and the jail and sheriff's office. The rest of that block, across the street from MacIver, included a barbershop and dentist's shop, a drygoods store, a bank, another hotel, and Turk Chaffee's saloon, which was the only saloon allowed on the west side of Bow Street. Chaffee's was small and subdued and genteel.

Across Third, still proceeding south along the west side of Bow, the pedestrian would pass a hardware store, a photographic gallery, a boardinghouse, the hospital of Dr. Nate Pohl, a restaurant, the offices of the Hilltop Mining Company—which was Guy Murvain—and then the Lodgepole Mining Company—which was the young and ambitious Pennsylvanian, Tom Larrabee.

Beyond Fourth Street, continuing south on his tour, the pedestrian would kick dust from his boots on the porch of the Crystal mine's office. Beyond that were the corrals and barn of a freight outfit, and then the theater, Nita Matlock's café where MacIver ate most of his meals, and the offices of three or four smaller mining companies that had shafts and tunnels higher up in the Yellows, to the east. Thereafter came another boardinghouse, a small hotel, a couple of warehouses and a number of private houses, and then the road to the Mexican Border eighty miles away.

Westward, in back of all those buildings fronting on the respectable side of Bow Street, were the houses and families of the town's self-styled better element. There were a few businesses and boardinghouses but most of that end of town was residential.

And that, MacIver reflected, was the decent side of Lodestar—the opposite side. Having taken his imaginary pedestrian on a tour of it, MacIver now imagined his pedestrian crossing the foot of Bow Street and coming back north along the near side—MacIver's side. Thirteen thousand people lived in this town and most of them lived on this side of it.

Madam Yvette's two-story house supported a chain-hung wooden sign, a little weatherbeaten, that said BOARDING FOR WOMEN. But that was not precisely what it meant. Coming up from Madam Yvette's, the pedestrian would pass a solid block of cribs, quiet, demure and plush of parlors. The more uproarious whorehouses were to be found back along King Street, a block east of Bow. Then, passing Fourth Street coming north toward MacIver's present position, the pedestrian would pass a bowling alley and a couple of small saloons and the Grand Hotel and Fry's Billiard Parlor and a few small shops. Then the pedestrian would cross the intersection and arrive here at the vast, ornate Nugget Saloon; and, if MacIver had his way, the pedestrian would stop right here and go inside.

Beyond the Nugget to the north was a gunshop and five saloons shoulder to shoulder. The block beyond was occupied by a café, three saloons, the livery stable and corrals, a feed store and a machinery and mining-supply company.

All of which was Bow Street. Behind it on the backside of town were the shacks where the miners lived, and the residences of freelance prostitutes and pimps and gamblers and bartenders, and a few small businesses.

And at the top of the hill, straddling the line that was Bow Street, stood Padre Ybarra's church.

If the imaginary pedestrian had seen all this, he would have seen Lodestar, Krayle MacIver's town. And it was MacIver's town in more than a figurative way. He owned a good deal of its real estate; as a matter of fact, he even owned the land on which the pious and pretentious National Hotel stood, at the head of the street. And, as owner of the Nugget—which was the town's biggest and wealthiest palace of entertainment—he was the leader of that group of men and madams who controlled the tough side of Lodestar. It was the tough side of Lodestar that owned the biggest population, most of the alcohol and gambling, and most of the women. The respectable folk on the genteel side of town across the street were people who bleated and complained and stood up self-righteously for law and order, peace and commerce, religion and propriety. But it was Krayle MacIver and those who stood at his shoulders who controlled Lodestar.

Over the peaks of the Yellows to the east, he saw the round thickness of thunderheads and the shadowed streaks of falling rain. The storm would reach Lodestar by nightfall, he knew, and he cursed mildly under his breath when he anticipated the foot-deep mud that the streets would become. Swamping out a saloon was an expensive job after a rain.

Up in that direction too, a mile away in the foothills, he saw the gentle rise of thick smoke from the Hilltop smelter. Hilltop, as well as the other mines, was running at full capacity these days. Miners worked around the clock in two twelve-hour shifts. The silver assayed almost three thousand dollars a ton, which was almost as high a grade of ore as Tombstone had produced in its heyday. MacIver had known Tombstone too, known it well, from '79 through '83, the peak years. Before that it had been Deadwood and Central City and Creed and Leadville. MacIver knew his mining towns and he knew where a profit lay—which was why he bought land and ran a fancy saloon instead of grubbing for gold or silver in the ground. He had his finger in a freighting business and another finger in a lumberyard and a third in the wholesale whiskey distribution for the area.

The cheroot was dry and hot in his mouth. He remembered Murphy, the miner dead in the street, and he remembered the cocky way Murphy's killer, Arnie, had walked away from the crowd. MacIver took the cheroot from his lips and tossed it into the dust of the street. Ashes scattered gently.

The light mud wagon stagecoach from Spanish Flat rocked around the corner of Second into Bow and pitched to a halt at the National Hotel, letting out a small group of passengers. Foot and horse and wagon traffic along the street was light; but it was drawing close to noon and MacIver knew that in another forty-five minutes the shifts would change at the mines. Then the town's pace would quicken.

Drawn by twelve teams of long-eared mules, a heavy wagon hauling ore tooled its ponderous way across Bow, down along Fourth, cutting across the intersection with the muleskinner riding the off-wheel mule and lifting his leather-throated voice against the animals. The buckboard from one of the up-valley ranches rolled in and stopped in front of the general mercantile, two cowboys riding the buckboard seat. MacIver watched the two cowboys walk inside the store; then he shook his shoulders to settle his coat and turned abruptly southwest, walking catty-corner across the intersection.

He walked south as far as Nita Matlock's café, and went in. It was five past twelve. In another half hour the place would be jammed with miners just down from the hill; but right now it was empty, altogether deserted except for Nita, who stood behind the counter wearing an apron and a pretty smile. Her tone was cheerful: "Good morning, Mr. MacIver."

A man of exactness, MacIver looked at his watch and said, "Good afternoon, Nita." He sat down at the oilcloth-covered counter and told her, "My usual lunch."

"Of course." She went back to the kitchen. MacIver sat on the stool leaning forward on his elbows; he lit a cigar and tilted it between his teeth and sat looking out through the dust-specked glass of the front window, at the street. A rider trotted past—Marla Searles, on her way out of town. MacIver ate his lunch at Nita's café every day at this precise time, and Marla knew it full well, but she didn't even glance toward the café. She was gone from sight quickly, but not quickly enough to keep MacIver's mind from jumping the straight track of his thoughts and following her. As long as he had known her, Marla had always been an enigma. Supple and soft and beautiful, she was at the same time as hard as any man and as shrewd. She was a match for MacIver if anyone in Lodestar was his match, and MacIver owned enough conceit not to acknowledge anyone else's superiority, publicly at least. He was not given to admitting his weaknesses to anyone; seldom did he admit them to himself.

Ostensibly Marla worked for him as a singer at the Nugget. In fact she owned a one-third share of the Nugget itself, but she wished to keep that ownership silent; and MacIver knew, though she had not spoken to him of it, that she was using her profits to buy into other businesses. She probably controlled more commerce in Lodestar than some of the more prominent businessmen from the other side of Bow Street.

Now and then he found a trace of faraway sadness in her glance, but it was only a superficial way she had of composing herself. Only once had he seen a real break in her iron reserve. She had come out of the Nugget one afternoon and accidentally encountered some of the ladies from the proper side of the line—ladies who held their heads high and their eyes haughtily averted and made a point of ignoring her. MacIver had seen her jaws bunch at the hinges; he had seen something in her eyes momentarily: perhaps injured pride, perhaps hate, perhaps envy, perhaps regret—he was not sure. But she had never lifted her guard again and never since then had he discovered any evidence of her emotions.

Long ago he had learned that he could approach no closer to her than a relationship of business partnership would allow; and since MacIver was a realist if nothing else, he had resigned himself to accepting that distance, and had sought his pleasures elsewhere. The pleasures Marla was willing to offer him were no more than what she would offer any man: the opportunity to watch the perfection of her beauty from afar.

He rose from the counter stool and walked unhurriedly to the door, opened it and tossed his half-consumed cigar out into the street's shifting dust. Then he shut the door and returned to his seat, and shortly thereafter Nita Matlock came forward from the kitchen with a plate of fried eggs and potatoes and a cup of black coffee, which she laid before him. He nodded and considered her casually. She was a tall girl, as tall as MacIver, which would make her five or six inches over five feet; she was slim and straight, with a gently strong body and firm round arms.

Her face was not at all beautiful; her lips were long, her eyes tilted slightly at the corners, her hair long and black. She smiled impersonally and went back toward the kitchen, no doubt to ready a tray of coffee cups for the impending swelling rush of miners.

MacIver forgot her then, as he forgot all unimportant thoughts, and put his mind on the question of Guy Murvain, boss of the Hilltop ventures, and Murvain's idea of sending for Ethan Scott. MacIver remembered once more the man Murphy, shot dead in the street not an hour ago, and when he coupled that thought with the image of Ethan Scott, the cold and implacable fighting man, he had to shake his head. One could fight fire with fire, or he could fight it with water. MacIver had seen enough violence to learn that it did not benefit business for long.

There was no question in MacIver's mind that the district was riddled with lawlessness. But the toughs, who were organized and led by Henry Dierkes, were only a secondary irritant to MacIver. His business had never suffered because of them, and if he were to look at it impartially, he would have to agree that the amount of money spent over his bar and gaming tables by Henry Dierkes and Dierkes's men made them valuable enough as customers.

Dierkes and his men, except for isolated incidents like this morning's shooting by Arnie, who was Dierkes's chief lieutenant—the toughs seldom troubled the town or the townspeople. It was the mines, the ranches, and the freight companies who suffered from the toughs, and this was what made Guy Murvain's hotheaded proposal seem unjust, to MacIver. Bringing Ethan Scott to Lodestar would bring headlines; and since MacIver had known Scott for a long time, he knew pretty well what the end result of Scott's coming would be: whether or not Scott successfully waged a campaign against Henry Dierkes and Dierkes's crew, the price of the battle—win or lose—would be paid by Lodestar more than it would be paid by the mines. On the face of it this was patently unfair, to MacIver's way of thinking. True, the mines supported the town; but at this moment, the toughs were hurting only the mines, and not the town. Personally, and as a business-man, MacIver had no animosity toward the toughs.

Neither was he troubled by a love for law and order. MacIver's position on this issue was dictated by a long life in frontier boom towns. He was a businessman of the frontier and the motives that moved him were motives of business profit. Experience had proved to him that the best and safest manner of making a profit was to live by the rough and crude codes of the frontier on which he made his living: to protect his own, by his own hand; to be honest in his dealings because it was profitable to be honest; to ask and give no quarter; and to mind his own affairs strictly.

More than once he had seen law and order come to a boom town. The result was inevitably one of two, each equally disastrous.

First came the rise of violence. The toughs and the law-and-order element quarreled and clashed. Sometimes it took the form of vigilante action, sometimes it was legalized through the deputization of hired gunfighters. This was the first in the series of acts. After the hiring would come the violence, the raw fighting, the grief. Men had to be hurt, men had to die. Then one side would emerge victorious. The toughs took over the town while the mines closed and the honest citizenry left, or the town would whip the toughs.

But when the town whipped the toughs, the town was no longer a boom town. Life became easygoing and well regulated by a body of enforcement officials. But lawlessness was a necessary ingredient for a boom. Once affairs were policed to the point of calm and safety, the whole boomtown rough-and-tumble atmosphere evaporated and with it went the elements that made big financial speculation possible, the kind of speculation MacIver pursued.

Once the toughs were driven from a town, the town turned against itself. Many a time MacIver had seen it come. The upstanding citizens in their flush of victory, and in their piety, rose up arrogantly to stamp out the undesir-ables in their midst. MacIver seldom had to remind himself that he was one of those undesirables. The town fought with all the insidious weapons at its command to rid itself of saloons and gambling halls and bawdy houses.

That was what came to a town with law and order. Perhaps it was the best end for the town's security-bent stable citizens, but it was not at all the best end for a restless gambler with his eye on the high stakes.

He finished his potatoes and attacked the eggs, pausing to sip coffee and look back over the years of his friendship with Ethan Scott. It was in spite of that friendship that he knew he could not support Murvain's plan or any plan like it. He was not yet ready for this town to die.

He finished his lunch, left a coin on the countertop, dipped his head to Nita and arrived back at the Nugget two minutes ahead of the crowd of miners. For a moment his eyes rested on the oil portrait of Marla above the bar; then he went back through the room to the watchman's pulpit and took a post there with his hand next to a loaded shotgun and his eyes on the crowd boiling in through the doorway.

III

"MY FRIEND," Eugenio Castillo said gently to Guy Murvain, "you can take your petty suspicions and roundabout accusations and peddle them somewhere else."

Murvain's brief smile was meant to placate the sheriff. "Look, Gene, you've got to admit that from where I stand it looks a bit peculiar."

"I don't stand where you do," the sheriff said. "But what's peculiar about it?"

Murvain clamped his mouth in an exasperated manner; he went to the door and looked out, as if to see if anyone were listening; and after he shut the door, he came back and sat down hipshot on the corner of the sheriff's desk. "Now, listen to me, Gene."

"Go right ahead," the sheriff said courteously. He half-concealed a yawn.

"It was me and the others who put you in office," Murvain said. "And we can easily enough get you out if we begin to think we should. And we're beginning to think so. A good many of my friends aren't too damned sure just which side you're on in this fracas."

"That's just what you said before," the sheriff said. His fat cheeks were flushed slightly darker than their normal tone. "Just what is it supposed to mean?"

"It means Henry Dierkes has been getting away with a good deal of mischief he shouldn't be able to get away with. It means that some of my fellow citizens are beginning to wonder if the reason why Dierkes finds it so easy to get away with mischief is because you make it easy for him."

"In other words," the sheriff said, "you think I've thrown in with Henry. Is that it?"

"Henry Dierkes has always been sort of a friend of yours, I believe." Murvain's tone was only mildly suggestive.

"He's a very likeable fellow," the sheriff murmured. "I have always gotten along well with him. So have most of the people in this country, except you and a few other stuffed shirts. Listen, my friend, and I'll tell you something: I am willing to bet that half the crimes you try to blame Henry for were committed by someone else. But as far as letting my personal friendships interfere with my job, that's something else again. You should know better." The silkiness of the sherriff's Spanish graced his speech.

"I felt I should warn you anyway," Murvain said stiffly. He crossed the office to the little chipped mirror on the wall by the door and stooped to look in the mirror. He adjusted his string tie and straightened his hat across his brows. He spoke again without turning: "There's going to be a council meeting this afternoon."

"I know."

"What they'll decide to do, I can't say. Public opinion to the contrary, I don't lead the council around by the nose."

"I know that too."

"Nobody leads the council around by the nose,"

Murvain went on, ignoring the sheriff's soft comment. "But I thought it fair to warn you that it's already been suggested that you step down and let Ethan Scott take your place as sheriff."

"Who suggested it?" the sheriff said immediately. "You?"

"No, not me. If you want to know, it was Tom Larrabee."

The sheriff shook his head sourly. "That young whelp."

"Young whelp or no, he swings a lot of weight. That Lodgepole mine of his is second in tonnage only to Hilltop—and I wouldn't forget that if I were you."

"Larrabee makes it difficult to forget it," the sheriff said. "He's disliked me ever since he came here. If he wants to oust me as sheriff, you and I both know why. I don't kow-tow to him. It's that simple. He expects every man to lower his eyes in his presence. I won't bow to any man, my friend."

"I know, I know," Murvain said soothingly. "But you may be in hot water, you know, and the only way to get out of it may be for you to show a little action. Now, if you were to bring in Henry Dierkes or a few of his boys. . . ."

"Cut it out," the sheriff said disgustedly. "You know my hands are tied. There's no proof against Henry and no witnesses against him for anything. What do you want me to arrest him for? Vagrancy?"

"That might do for a start," Murvain said, and smiled grimly. "You think about it, Gene." He palmed the knob and turned outside.

When the door clicked shut, Sheriff Castillo's face lowered into a frown and he rammed one fist gently into the other palm. He pushed himself to his feet with effort and waddled back through the cellblock corridor to the back door of the jail, and went out into the alley. The sun smote him; dust smell was strongly acrid in the hot air. He walked up the alley to the back of the National Hotel and across the head of the street, below the Church, to the Ace Livery Barn, where he picked up his horse and mounted, and rode out of the stable.

He was about to turn away from the stable mouth when a pedestrian coming along the street hailed him, and he neck-reined the horse around to see who it was. The man coming forward was Tom Larrabee, and the sheriff's lips moved briefly with his breathing: *"Diciendo al diablo!"*

"Taking a ride?" Larrabee inquired smoothly.

The sheriff nodded slightly.

"Hot day for travel," Larrabee observed.

"A mite hot," the sheriff agreed with some reserve. Larrabee grinned at him. The sheriff said, "I hear you've had some words to say about me."

"Do you?"

"Whenever you think you can fill my boots," the sheriff said softly, "you're welcome to try, my friend."

"It shouldn't be hard," Larrabee said, still smiling. "But I probably wouldn't try to balance on the fence as much as you do."

The sheriff frowned; but Larrabee only smiled lazily once more, said a murmured "Good luck," and turned away. A little puzzled, the sheriff turned his mount and rode out of town eastward toward the Yellows with his head tipped toward his massive chest.

Henry Dierkes rummaged through his wooden trunk and brought out a pair of black broadcloth trousers. Still shirtless, he stropped up his razor and lathered his face. In the mirror on the sagging door, he saw a belyingly cheerful and easygoing face belonging to a man of strong ambition whom chance had steered onto the wrong trails; he saw a man of disguised and mottled past, many regrets and none but an uncertain future. But he grinned—it was his habit to grin. He was tall and brick red of hair, and were it not for his abundant brown freckles and the knobby break at the bridge of his nose, he would have been good-looking. He was long and lean from a life of horseback travel and his hands were calloused and scarred; and his gunbelt had a well used look.

He wiped the razor, laid it back on the shelf and used last night's shirt to rub his face; he muttered a quiet tune:

Oh, my name it is Sam Hall, it is Sam Hall.
Oh, my name is Samuel Hall, Samuel Hall.
Well, my name it is Sam Hall,

And I hate you one and all,
Oh, I hate you one and all,
God damn your eyes.

Thereupon he gave the dismal room a short, contemptuous scrutiny. The empty whiskey bottle reminded him of the room's stale whiskey smell and he went to the door to open it and clear out that mustiness; he blinked against the brightness of the noonday sky, even though it was clouded over, and stood looking out a moment.

Oh, I killed a man, they say, so they say.
Oh, I killed a man, they say, so they say.
I knocked him on the head,
And I left him lie there dead,
Yes, I left him lie there dead,
God damn his eyes.

His voice cracked on the high notes. He turned back inside the cabin. Gray light filtered weakly through the spattered panes of the windows, listlessly revealing dust on the floor and on the furniture. There were wide cracks in the chinking of the walls. He put on a clean shirt and went out into the yard, slightly hung over and without some of his usual good cheer. Rain began falling in small drops, coming from the higher mountain chains to the east. He called: "Arnie!"

Arnie was often too independent for Dierkes's taste. Now Arnie did not appear. Dierkes's restless temper rose a bit as he wondered where his home crew was. He swore and returned to the cabin, humming the melody of "Sam Hall," and spilled flour, eggs and milk into a frying pan. He heated up the potbellied stove and stood watching the red glow in the stove's square isinglass window, waiting impatiently for the flapjacks to cook.

Oh, they tried me in the town, in the town.
Yes, they tried me in the town, in the town.
And the judge, he shook his head,
He said, "Hang him till he's dead."

Oh, he said, "Hang him till he's dead,"
God damn his eyes.

Oh, the parson he did come, he did come.
Yes the parson he did come, he did come.
And he looked so long and glum
When he talked of Kingdom Come,
I was wishin' he'd get done,
God damn his eyes.

And the sheriff he came too, he came too.
Yes, the sheriff he came too, he came too.
With his men all dressed in blue,
And full of mountain dew,
Well, they were a drunken crew,
God damn their eyes.

He took a pacing turn around the room, humming,
and paused by the window, watching the buildup of storm
clouds overhead and to the east. The main body of his
crew of toughs was camped back in Peacock Gorge, ten
miles farther up in the Yellows, and by now they would be
feeling the brunt of the westering thunderstorm. In another hour it would be here in full force. Dierkes shook his
head, trying to clear the fuzz from it. When he returned to
the stove he lifted the frying pan, dropped it heavily on
the table and cursed as he rubbed his burned hand against
his trouser leg. He got a fork and bit into the meal without
much hunger, wishing he had had the sense last night to
leave a few swallows in the whiskey bottle. The pancakes
were dry and tasteless but he ate them because he was a
lean man, an active man who used his energy rapidly and
needed to replenish it regularly. He finished the meal
quickly, grimaced, rose from the table and left the cabin
again. He stood under the scant shelter of the roof over-
hang and regarded the dismally dripping rain.

Now up the rope I go, up I go.
Well, up the rope I go, up I go.
And those bastards down below,
They're saying, "Sam, we told you so,"

They're saying, "Sam, we told you so,"
God damn their eyes.

But now in Heaven I dwell, in Heaven I dwell.
Yes, now in Heaven I dwell, in Heaven I dwell;
Yes, now in Heaven I dwell,
And I've been here for a spell,
And all those bums are down in Hell,
God damn their eyes.

"And thus ending the morning prayer," Dierkes murmured, "the parson went about his daily chores. Come now, brethren!"

Hoofbeats patted the ground from somewhere lower down and Dierkes stood in the yard, waiting. It sounded like a single rider. His hands touched his guns. He watched the mountains dropping steeply off at the foot of the yard and when a rider appeared from the nearest fringe of lodgepole timber, he relaxed and folded his arms. That was Arnie. Arnie rode forward at a steady gait, dismounted by the corral and led his horse inside. He unsaddled and brushed down the animal; all this while Dierkes stood waiting silently. Then Arnie came across the yard, rain speckling his hat, and Dierkes said, "Where've you been?"

"In town," Arnie said shortly.

"You're jumpy," Dierkes observed. "Trouble?"

"Murphy," Arnie said, nodding.

"Who's Murphy?"

"One of the Hilltop miners. He called me names and drew a gun on me."

"I rise to remark," Dierkes said, "that your health looks good enough. Murphy must have missed."

"He did."

"And you?"

"I didn't miss," Arnie said.

"Anybody ask questions?"

"Castillo cleared me. He wants me to testify at the coroner's hearing, that's all."

Dierkes nodded. "Just the same, be more careful to stay out of trouble in town."

"Hell," Arnie said irritably, "I didn't start it." He

swung past Dierkes into the cabin, and soon after his departure the sound of advancing hoofs again arrested Henry Dierkes, and once more Dierkes touched his guns. Arnie came out of the cabin to stand beside him, squat and powerful. Arnie's tone was petulant. "I didn't know you'd drunk up all the hooch."

"Sorry," Dierkes answered drily. His eyes lay against the timber eastward, toward the higher mountains. In time two horsemen came into view, threading the trees, and broke into the yard at a walk. This was Dierkes's home crew.

The Mex, riding in the lead, was a young man who had ridden with Dierkes off and on for a few years, and who had never bothered to announce his name. Therefore he was known simply as the Mex. The Mex had an antelope tied across his saddle, all spotted fur and eyes and matted blood. "Give me a hand here, Raven."

Raven stepped down from his saddle, paused briefly to lay his malevolently expressionless glance against Arnie and Henry Dierkes, and came around to help the Mex undo the lashings on the antelope carcass. Where Arnie was squat and puff-cheeked, Raven was gaunt and hollow, an ex-Texas badman recently of Tombstone. Raven wore a ragged, sickly beard, and where his cheeks showed, flesh was a stretched parchment reluctantly bulging here and there to allow space for bones.

These four men filed inside the cabin, the Mex in the lead carrying the dead antelope. Rain fell in the yard with increasing pressure; the clouds were slate gray. On the cabin floor the Mex fell to with his knife, a young and dark man with a blandly innocent face. Arnie was building a fire up in the stove; afterward he hunkered by it, holding his hands toward the warmth, palms out. "Cold up here. I could use a bottle of rye." His eyes lifted to the empty bottle on the table, and then flicked Henry Dierkes; but Arnie made no further comment. It was Raven who spoke; he whirled back from the door, his gaunt frame held in a tight, strained way. "Damn it, shut up, Arnie." Raven was cruel and harsh and rashly primitive; he was a haunted man.

"Simmer down," Henry Dierkes murmured, watching Raven with a narrowed glance, not trusting the man at all.

Raven ignored him. Raven's attention had shifted to the Mex: "Hurry up with the carvin' there—I'm hungry."

The Mex looked up bleakly, making no answer. He picked up the antelope's hide and went outside with it, and a moment later returned empty-handed. Henry Dierkes put his hat on and walked to the door; he stood in the opening looking out at the drizzling rain, hearing Arnie's murmured talk cutting across the air lazily behind him: "You're an artist with that knife, kid."

"Sure," the Mex replied, and though Dierkes was not looking that way, he felt the Mex's glance tight against Raven. Dierkes turned his head abruptly, so as to catch them unawares, and found he was right. The gaunt gunfighter was matching the Mex's hot stare but neither of them spoke a word; and after a moment the Mex's eyes pulled away, demonstrating more clearly than any talk that Raven was the deadlier man. The Mex cut a haunch from the meat, speared it on a stick and held it in the stove's fire, turning it slowly, sitting on his heels with his hat pulled low over his face to shield it from the red heat. Raven's evil countenance stood motionless in a dim corner, hovering; and Arnie, the squat one, completed the triangle by stretching out on Dierkes's unmade bunk, seemingly unconcerned by Raven's display of bullying. Then, abruptly, Dierkes wheeled outside to look around. His voice carried back over his shoulder: "Somebody's coming. Heads up—heads up."

Everyone moved, out of habit and experience. Arnie, first to react, leaped off the bunk and strode to the door to pick up his rifle, which he had left leaning by the jamb. Back in the room, Raven crossed to the open window and stood there with his fist closed around the handle of his gun. The Mex looked up, blank of expression, but did not remove the meat from the fire. Henry Dierkes stepped ahead into the rain. "Only one rider," he decided; "you boys can relax."

"We'll see," Arnie murmured, and went softly across the dripping yard to the shadows of the barn, dragging his rifle.

Dierkes turned to speak over his shoulder: "Raven."
"What?"

"Keep your gun holstered unless I give the word."

Raven's answer came from the cabin, dry and reluctant: "All right."

Then Dierkes swung his tall frame forward to face the head of the trail, and waited.

Rain made shadows of everything. Yonder horseman advanced without hurry, his horse's hoofs throwing up clots of mud, and presently Henry Dierkes relaxed, recognizing the fat figure of the oncoming rider. He spoke shortly: "It's all right."

Raven came out of the doorway behind him; Raven was coughing with a rattle, bent over his hollow chest. Raven said, "Who says it's all right? I don't cotton to his kind."

"When you're runnin' this outfit," Dierkes drawled with lazy contempt, "then you can give orders. Meanwhile drift over to the barn and keep Arnie company. Make sure there's no company on the sheriff's trail."

Raven moved away, his face dark and mean, and soon the sheriff dismounted in the yard, left his horse's reins to trail, and waddled forward past Dierkes into the cabin, where he removed his hat and flowing yellow slicker and shook his head violently like a wet dog. His fat jowls wobbled; droplets of water splashed around. Dierkes followed him inside. "Leave us alone," he said to the Mex, and waited until the Mex had gone. Then he sat down at the table and watched the sheriff. "Bad weather for travel."

"Sure," the sheriff said. "It was a dreary ride." He sat down opposite Dierkes and pulled makings out of a pocket and proceeded to spin up a cigarette.

"What's wrong?"

"Maybe nothing," the sheriff said. "Hard to tell. But I've got one little piece of news for you."

"Well?"

"Murvain's getting smart. His payroll won't be coming in on a wagon this time. It will be on the stagecoach— tomorrow, the noon stage from Spanish Flat. Three months' payroll. Almost thirty thousand dollars."

Dierkes nodded. "That's good," he said. "We'll have to take that."

"It won't be too easy. There will be armed guards on

the coach and a posse of a dozen or more miners riding about five minutes behind the stage, armed to the teeth."

Dierkes shrugged. "I never met a dirt-digger yet that could hit the broad side of a barn from inside the barn."

"These can," the sheriff said. "Murvain picked men who can shoot."

"Then we'll find a way around them. Shouldn't take five minutes to finish the job."

"Why not let it go, let Murvain cool down a little?"

"I can't," Dierkes said.

"Hell," the sheriff grunted, "what's so important about one payroll?"

"I have the feeling," Dierkes replied abstractedly, "that we've got Murvain where we want him—on the downhill ski. His insurance brokers are about ready to cancel his contract."

"What of it?"

"Nothing—forget it. Let's just say I want to break Guy Murvain."

"What for? What did he ever do to you?"

Dierkes shook his brick-topped head. "Let's drop the subject. Look, what's this about Arnie shooting a man?"

"Self-defense. An open-and-shut case."

"You're sure?"

"I'm sure."

"All right," Dierkes said. "Damn it, I don't have a single man around here I can trust. I've even got to ask *you* about Arnie."

The sheriff grinned comfortably. "Hell of a note, ain't it, Henry?"

Dierkes grimaced. He glanced at the empty whiskey bottle centered on the table; he picked it up and aimed at the paneless window and let fly. The bottle sailed through and disappeared, and smashed with a sharp tinkling of glass on the ground outside. The sheriff said, "You're as jumpy as I am, ain't you?"

"What have you got to be jumpy about?"

The sheriff's smile went away. "There's a council meeting going on right now. They don't know anything, but I get it in the way some of them look at me—they don't trust me any more. They're fed up with you getting away with everything. They don't like my brand of law enforcement. It may be they're almost ready to chuck me."

"I see," Dierkes said. "Then what? No law at all?"

"There's talk of hiring Ethan Scott."

It brought Dierkes all the way down from his detached amusement. "What?"

"Ethan Scott," the sheriff said.

Dierkes said, "I don't like that."

"Fine," the sheriff said. "Fine and dandy. But if they're set to do it, there ain't much we can do to stop them, now is there?"

"Maybe—maybe." Dierkes's voice was quiet. Then he looked up. "When's he due to arrive?"

"Murvain sent a telegram to Tucson yesterday. No telling how long it'll take to catch up with Scott, and then there's no telling whether Scott will take the job. There's one thing in our favor."

"And?"

"Murvain's mad, but he thinks I'm all right. He'll ʜide with me. It may be enough to keep me in office. They may just hire Scott as a mine combine agent, not a law officer. They might have a little trouble pinning a badge on him—I understand he's been in and out of the pokey a few times."

Dierkes nodded. "He has. I spent a year at Yuma with him."

The sheriff's eyebrows lifted. "What was he in for?"

"Manslaughter," Dierkes said drily. "It was after he was marshal of Careyville. The population let him go ahead and clean up the town and make everything peaceful. Then they discovered they had a bull by the tail and they suddenly wanted to get rid of him. He'd done their dirty work for them, but they weren't grateful to him for it, not a bit. Honest folks seldom are."

"What happened?"

"He owned some property there. He didn't want to leave, but the good upstandin' citizens decided to push him a little. He pushed back. I guess maybe they were a little ashamed of him. They pinned a manslaughter charge on him and sent him off to Yuma. It worked all right. He sold all his property in that town and never went back."

Dierkes threw his head back in laughter; and after a moment he said, "And who is it that preaches about lovin' thy neighbor?"

"I reckon," the sheriff agreed morosely. "But right now it's beside the point. If I lose my job, things will get a lot harder for both of us."

Dierkes grinned. "Want me to ride into Lodestar and tell everybody why they should keep you in office?"

The sheriff did not match his grin. "Tom Larrabee's doing his best to shove me out of my job."

Dierkes sobered and leaned forward, speaking quietly. "Don't worry about Tom Larrabee," he said. "Not ever."

"What?"

The sheriff's head moved uncertainly. "There's more than one talking against me. If you get away with that stagecoach payroll tomorrow, they'll for damn sure kick me out."

"Then we'll frame it on somebody," Dierkes said. "Don't worry about it—you won't lose face. I'll leave plenty of evidence around to point where we want it to."

"Where?"

Dierkes ignored the interruption. "All you'll have to do is follow it up. I'll plant some of the money. You'll be a hero. Nobody will think of firing you after tomorrow."

"But who gets framed?"

"Leave that to us," Dierkes said. "Now I think you'd better get back to your office before somebody wonders where you've been all this time."

"Yeah," the sheriff said, frowning uncertainly. "Sure." And with a single baffled shake of his fat face, he left.

As soon as the sheriff was gone from the yard, Dierkes went to the barn and spoke to the Mex: "You can go back inside and cook that antelope haunch now. But saddle my horse first."

And then, in the driving rain, he rode downslope toward the lower foothills of the Yellows—westward. It was a two-hour ride to his destination and he knew he would be late, but he expected her to be there anyway, and she was.

This far down toward the valley it was not raining yet. He had left the storm half an hour back in the hills above;

and now, with his poncho folded and tied across the back of his saddle, he halted carefully atop a bald hill to survey the roundabout slopes, and seeing nothing dangerous there, he put his horse down into the green hollow below. It was a pretty little canyon, stream-fed with a line of marching cottonwoods marking the path of the creek. He threaded a field of brown-eyed yellow daisies and entered the trees, and rode forward parallel to the river bank until he came to the bend in the stream, and found her there waiting for him.

She was dismounted; her horse was tied to a nearby cottonwood and she sat in a small patch of sunlight, her legs crossed Indian-fashion, rolling a cigarette in the best accepted masculine manner. Her beauty took his breath. She looked up, moving her face in a lazy way, and smiled vaguely. Dierkes stepped down, left his horse ground-hitched, and strode forward on his long legs. She didn't rise, and so after a moment's silence he sat down by her. She said, "You're a little late, aren't you?"

"Had a visitor. Held me up."

"The sheriff?"

He gave no sign that she had surprised him; he only said, "What gives you that idea?"

She smiled. "Don't worry—I can keep a secret."

"You see a lot, don't you?" he said.

Her supple shoulders lifted and dropped. She had her cigarette lit and she lay back on her elbows, watching the smoke rise in thin streaks that fled with the breeze. Dierkes rolled over and pushed her down flat and dropped his mouth over her lips, just that abruptly. She lay motionless under him. Her lips were warm and moist; her hands moved up his back and she pressed him to her, gently. He felt the soft contours of her body throb under him and when he lifted his head he said, "I don't get it."

"What?"

"You could have Krayle MacIver without lifting a finger. Why me? MacIver's a better bet than I am."

She smiled, a slow upturning of her lip corners. "Most men would try to avoid that kind of thinking."

"That's no answer," he said. "What's wrong with MacIver?"

"I don't need a man with money. I can make all the money I want for myself."

"So?"

"So take away Krayle's money. What's left?"

"Well," he said slowly, "you tell me."

She moved her head back and forth along the ground. "He's a runt."

"So was Napoleon. I wouldn't underestimate MacIver."

"Don't ask for explanations," she said. "Maybe you remind me of someone—someone with guts. Maybe it's something else. I can't give you a cut-and-dried answer. You and I, we get along together—isn't that enough?"

"Why," he said, "I suppose it is. But just don't give MacIver an idea of what's going on between us."

"My private life is none of Krayle's business. He knows that."

"Sure," Dierkes said. "But just the same I kind of like him."

"He won't find out," Marla answered. Her tone was low and throaty; he lowered his head again for her kiss.

IV

NORMALLY KRAYLE MACIVER was as even-tempered as any man might be expected to be, but this afternoon the presence of Tom Larrabee irritated him to the point of jabbing a remark at Larrabee: "I observed you didn't fight too damn hard to get Castillo ousted. Changing your mind about him?"

Larrabee just glanced at him, and MacIver said, "I never yet heard you admit a mistake. I guess I didn't really expect it now."

"You're not quite as funny as you like to think," Larrabee answered. He looked more directly at MacIver, and presently shrugged noncommittally; he preceded MacIver into the Nugget and pushed a path through the crowd to the bar. MacIver followed him, making use of the avenue created by Larrabee's arrogantly shoving shoulders and elbows. Then the two men stood at the bar over whiskey glasses, MacIver a head shorter than his companion, and Larrabee said, "You don't like me."

"Not particularly. Why should I?"

"A lot of people seem to think it's politic to like me." Larrabee's lazy smile was full of dry amusement.

"I never have liked roughshod men," MacIver answered.

Larrabee didn't take offense. He was tall and husky, a block-jawed young man with obvious, energetic ambition pushing him relentlessly. His eyes brooded darkly at all times. He said now, almost by way of defense, "I've never thought much of Gene Castillo. I think he's a soft fat man doing a soft fat job. We need somebody tougher than he is in the sheriff's office. But I haven't got anything specific on Castillo. That's why I didn't put up a big fight to get him fired. Satisfied?"

MacIver watched him speculatively; then, after a moment, he said, "Why not?" and turned to his glass. He stared down at it, watching the whiskey turn brown and amber and brown again, and wondered what was keeping Marla out so late in the afternoon. Tom Larrabee's voice drifted quietly across his thoughts: "Well, it sure as hell was a long enough meeting."

"It was," MacIver agreed without attention.

"You sort of got outvoted on the question of hiring Ethan Scott," Larrabee said, smiling politely to take the sting out of the contempt in his talk.

MacIver shrugged in answer; he doffed his hat, handed it to the bartender to be put away, and ran fingers through his steel-gray hair while he put an elbow on the bar and turned to look over the crowd. Half the tables were busy; later on, after the supper hour, the whole floor would be crowded. The piano player—the "professor"—was banging on the out-of-tune keys and some of the hired girls, rouged and coldly smiling, danced with the grimly plodding miners who paid half a dollar a dance. Tom Larrabee's idle talk cut forward once more: "I guess you can't win all the time."

"No," MacIver said. He frowned slightly, buried in his thoughts, and sipped whiskey from his glass.

He had let the conversation drop, but Larrabee revived it: "You don't like the idea of bringing in Ethan Scott. Why?"

"I think it spells the end of this town." MacIver made his brief statement, and caught Larrabee's impatient, shrewd glance studying him; and suddenly Larrabee said, "Then you might be wanting to pull up stakes, if you think the town's about to die."

"Maybe," MacIver replied cautiously.

"I was thinking about the land on Bow Street where the National Hotel stands."

MacIver lifted an eyebrow at him. "I see," he said.

"I still want to buy it. A few months ago I offered you eight thousand for the land. It's a good offer. It still stands."

"With the mines losing every other payroll, where do you get that kind of money?"

Larrabee smiled shortly. "That's the insurance company's loss, not mine. How about it?"

MacIver thought about it. "I want to watch some of the fun," he said. "After all, the town won't dry up and blow away overnight."

Larrabee just stood with as patient an expression as he could muster. MacIver thought of the impending arrival of Ethan Scott and all that it meant or could mean to him; and presently he said, "All right. You have a bargain."

"Good."

"Let's go back to my office and I'll make out a bill of sale, and transfer the deed to you."

Larrabee followed him across the length of the room to a door where MacIver produced a key, stooped by the keyhole to insert it, and went on through. He went to his desk, and around it, and knelt on one knee by the safe in the corner. He spun the combination dial and swung the heavy door open. "That's an impressive-looking safe," Tom Larrabee said. MacIver grunted, shuffling documents, and after a moment found the deed to the land Larrabee wanted. He locked the safe again and took the deed to his desk. Larrabee stood with his arms folded, looking aimlessly out the back window into the alley, lips pursed in soundless whistling. MacIver filled out the deed and made out a bill of sale and said, "Let's go over to the bank."

"All right."

MacIver locked the door behind him, and they returned to the saloon. Then the two of them went outside and crossed the street to the Merchant's Bank. Larrabee wrote out a draft, received an incurious look from the teller, waited for the cashier to pass his draft, and turned the cash over to MacIver without counting it. MacIver took the time to tally it. "Eight thousand," he said, nodding perfunctorily, and put the bills away in his pocket. "A drink?"

"No," Larrabee said. "But I'll join you for supper."

MacIver glanced at him but declined to comment. He led the way outside once more and down Bow Street as far as Nita Matlock's café. There was a small crowd in the place but they found an unoccupied table near the back corner, and sat. MacIver watched Larrabee with a speculative gaze, wondering at the man's sudden sociability. They gave their orders to Nita and then, after a stretching interval of silence, Larrabee said, "You wouldn't have sold me this land if you didn't really think the ship was about to sink."

"Maybe," MacIver answered. "Or maybe I just doubt I'll ever get more than eight thousand for that piece of land."

"I'm inclined to disagree."

"Obviously."

Larrabee's nervous smile removed a few of the rough angles from his face. When Nita came forward with two cups of coffee, Larrabee looked up at her pretty dark head and said, "I'll take you to the theater Saturday, Nita."

She shook her head gently. "I'm sorry. I can't, Tom."

Then she turned away, busy, and MacIver caught the ugly look passing briefly across Larrabee's cheeks. Larrabee was plainly a man of strong and unchecked feelings, tough and smart with more than his share of drive. It struck MacIver that Larrabee was a dangerous man in a position to make grief for a great many people if he so chose; and it occurred to MacIver that it might be wise to keep a finger on Larrabee's pulse in the future. But when he spoke he displayed none of this. He said in an idle way, "A man wonders where a man as young as you would get enough money to start a big operation like Lodgepole."

Larrabee's reply was equally at ease. "It's a mistake to think youth or age has anything to do with a man's ability."

"Maybe—maybe. But it takes a certain amount of time to accumulate money."

"Not you. Why not me?"

"I see," MacIver said. Larrabee was making it plain enough he didn't want to reveal the sources of his fortune; and while this reluctance made MacIver a little more suspicious, it also told him it would probably be wise not to press the subject.

Larrabee leaned forward, his young face tightened for emphasis. MacIver wondered idly how old he really was. Twenty-four? Larrabee was saying: "A man's a hammer or he's an anvil. That's plain. Right at the beginning he's got to decide which he's going to be."

"And you decided to be the hammer."

"That's it," Larrabee breathed. He was so grimly serious that MacIver was half frightened and half tempted to laugh outright. Larrabee said, "Once a man makes that decision, he's got to move ahead in a straight line. He can't allow anything or anybody to get in his way. If they do...."

Larrabee didn't have to finish. MacIver finished for him: "They get stepped on."

"Exactly. If you don't step on them they'll step on you. So you climb all over them if you have to—but you get to the top."

"Hoping all the while," MacIver murmured, "that the fellows you stepped on won't reach up and pull you down."

"They can't," Larrabee said, evenly enough. "Not if you've stepped on them hard enough."

"I see," MacIver said softly. "That's a pretty hard philosophy you've got there, my friend."

Larrabee only smiled a tight little smile. "Maybe. It's a good one—it works. That's all that counts."

"Sure," MacIver answered. But his thoughts disagreed. *Is it? Well, maybe it is. But every time I've seen a man like you, my friend, he's turned out to be a man who wanted to reach just a little too far—and fell off in the trying.* Too much ambition could be as harmful as too much of anything else. But for the moment he said nothing; he only wondered. Of all the mines on the slopes of the Yellows, the two most powerful were Murvain's Hilltop and Larrabee's Lodgepole. That made Larrabee a big frog in the pond. How much bigger did he intend to grow?

The next afternoon MacIver returned to Lodestar on his rented horse. A deep and puzzled frown crossed his face. At two-thirty by his watch he left the horse at the Ace Livery Barn and paused on the sidewalk to read the note again, for what must have been the tenth time:

"If you want to know what Marla Searles does all the time when she's out riding then meet me at one-thirty at the foot of the Hilltop wagon road."

The note wasn't signed; it was printed in pencil. He shook his head, baffled, and pocketed the note. Then he walked down Bow to the Nugget and swung angrily through the almost empty saloon to his office. He unlocked the door and went inside, looked at the note again, and tossed it on the desk. He had kept the appointment, out of admitted curiosity, but no one had met him. After waiting half an hour he had come back to town, bewildered and half disgusted.

Now, with other things on his mind, he put the note in a desk drawer and turned to the safe. One chore he hated was paperwork, but the books had to be kept up to date. Outside, through the open window, he heard a small commotion up the street. It sounded like a number of men shouting from the vicinity of the National Hotel. He stopped to listen, and heard enough of the scattered phrases to get the idea that the noon stage from Spanish Flat, carrying Murvain's big Hilltop payroll, had been held up on the Coach Road.

MacIver frowned, devoted a moment's thought to stage holdups and lawlessness in general, and returned to the safe, spinning the combination dial back and forth and swinging the heavy iron door open. His books were leather-bound, wide and flat, and he reached in for them. But then sight of something else, something foreign in his safe, arrested him, and he reached in.

When he brought his hand out, grasped in it was a small canvas sack with a black stenciled stamp: HILLTOP COMPANY.

He looked at it blankly, not knowing what to make of it, and pulled the drawstrings open to look inside. What he saw there dumbfounded him even more.

The sack contained money. When he took it out and counted it he found it totaled exactly three thousand dollars. He scratched his head and looked up, and noticed the shouting still going on in the street.

And then he knew, suddenly and all at once, and heard the run of his own muffled cursing. He understood abruptly what the money was doing in his safe, and why he had received the anonymous note. It was simple and yet effective; it was as well planned a frame-up as he had heard of. Undoubtedly one of the stagecoach robbers had dressed in clothes like MacIver's and made himself visible to the stage passengers. Meanwhile the anonymous note had tolled MacIver out of town, making sure the office would be empty for the planting of the evidence, and making sure MacIver didn't have an adequate alibi for the time of the stage holdup.

He shook his head, part in admiration, part in wonder, and part in anger; and then, suddenly, he knew he had to get rid of the money before the passengers' story would lead the sheriff here. He would leave it till later to determine how the thieves had opened his safe, and why they had chosen him as their scapegoat.

He slammed the safe door and spun the dial; he put the sack of money inside his coat, dipped his head and climbed out through the window, dropping a brief four feet to the alley dust. He walked casually down the alley to King Street and went north a block and a half to First, and turned left past the livery corrals to the corner of Bow, where he stood in the shadows to scout the street. Down by the sheriff's office the stagecoach was drawn up and a sizable crowd of men surrounded it. Up on the walk he saw the sheriff's massive shape; the sheriff lifted his thick arms and launched into a short speech, after which the crowd began to disperse. The sheriff started walking south with determined step, obviously headed for the Nugget, and MacIver kept his post until the knot of men had broken apart, its fragments scattering along the street; and then, walking casually, he crossed the head of Bow Street in plain sight, passing the church door, and went along behind the National Hotel after pausing by the corner to see if anyone abroad had recognized him. There was no hue and cry; he presumed therefore that he had not been seen. He went around the hotel and cruised down the alley behind it, crossed Second Street and put himself thereby immediately behind the jail. He grinned tightly at the barred, high window; he took the sack of Hilltop money from his coat, glanced both ways to make sure the alley was deserted, and tossed the money sack inside through the window.

He needed time to think, and so he continued down the alley across Third and Fourth, and when he found himself behind the freight yards of the Lodgepole Mining Company—Tom Larrabee's outfit—he stopped in the shade of a wagon ramada and stood frowning at the dusty toes of his boots, thinking back.

It was the proximity of the freight yards that made him think of Tom Larrabee, and that thought in turn made him remember that last night Larrabee had been in his office with him. Larrabee had, in fact, been present while MacIver opened the safe to get out the deed to the land Larrabee had bought. It wasn't far from there to the hypothesis that Larrabee had entered his office last night for the express purpose of watching him open the safe, to learn the combination. Then, after the stage holdup, someone had brought a small part of the loot—the sack of Hilltop payroll money—and climbed in the window, caching the money in MacIver's safe.

It had been nicely done, MacIver admitted. It was only the bandits' bad luck that they hadn't known he would be opening the safe to do his books today.

Decision crystallized in his mind and he climbed through the corral fence into the Lodgepole yard, crossed the corral, not bothering to hide, and entered the back door of the tackroom. He walked straight on through and opened the front door without hesitating. The door led to the front office, as he knew; and Tom Larrabee's desk was up front by the window.

Larrabee's head whirled and his eyes opened a little wider; his flesh paled. Then the young man took hold of himself, casting a blank curtain across his expression and sitting back. MacIver shut the door quietly behind him and leaned indolently against it. Larrabee swallowed; his Adam's apple bobbed; he said, "What are you doing here?"

"I just wanted to ask a few friendly questions."

"Then why not try the front door?"

"Bad for my health," MacIver said in a tone as tight as his balled fists. "Why did you try to frame me on the stage holdup?"

"Why what?"

Larrabee's surprise was so complete it seemed genuine; MacIver's assurance faltered. He said, "I got rid of the money. All your work of planting it went to no good. They can't pin anything on me without evidence."

"Pin what on you? What money? Who planted what? MacIver, what in hell is wrong with you?"

"You watched me open my safe last night," MacIver said. "You saw the combination. You're the only one who could have opened it."

"Are you accusing me of rifling your safe?"

"No."

Larrabee frowned deeply and leaned forward against his wide, heavy desk. "Look, I don't have the slightest notion of what you're talking about, but if you think I'm the only man who could get into your safe, you're out of your mind. I've noticed several times how careless you are with that thing. I've even mentioned it a few times, to Murvain and Sheriff Castillo and others. Ask them, if you don't believe me. Hell, I've been in your office a half dozen times while you opened that safe. So have any number of people. Why accuse me?"

MacIver hesitated. He stood by the tackroom door with his hand under his coat near the butt of his little birdhead Colt, and frowned forward at Larrabee, trying to make up his mind, trying to find the truth. And at last he knew Larrabee was right. He had jumped to the conclusion that Larrabee had framed him, because Larrabee had been with him last night. But it was probably true that a good many people could have got the combination to his safe during the past months. And it was plain that any one of them could have planned this frame-up. He had, he realized abruptly, gone off half-cocked—and it was unlike his nature to do that. The frame had rattled him, but it shouldn't have disturbed him so badly he couldn't think right. He was ashamed of his act, and he removed his hand from his coat, and made his apology, as lucidly as he could; and when he had apologized, Larrabee watched him with a suspicious glance. "Maybe you'd better tell me what this is all about."

MacIver shook his head. "I don't think so," he said. "Someone did me a rotten turn, and I figured it must have been you. I was wrong. I'm sorry I bothered you." He turned quickly and went out through the same back door through which he had entered; and when he achieved the alley behind Larrabee's corral, he stood undecided a moment. Then he shrugged his shoulders to settle his coat, and went around the end of the alley, making his way back through town to the Nugget.

As he had anticipated, the sheriff was there, just now coming forward from the bar with an angry scowl. The sheriff's fat face was flushed with heat; the leather sweat of saddle travel was a stench on him. "I want to talk to you, Señor."

The sheriff had a habit, MacIver knew, of lapsing into Spanish phrasings when he was angry. But it would do to soothe the sheriff just now. "Come back to the office," MacIver said smoothly, and led the way without awaiting the sheriff's reply.

He stopped by his desk and turned in time to see the sheriff marching grimly ahead through the door. The sheriff closed the door, whirled and said, "Take off your coat, please."

"What?"

"Take off your coat, Señor."

MacIver looked at him, astonished; but he obeyed the

sheriff's command. The sheriff grunted. "Now take off your vest and shirt."

MacIver colored. He answered hotly: "Now, wait a minute. . . ."

"Damn it, do as I say!"

MacIver's lips tightened into a grimace. He unbuckled his shoulder-holster and set it on the desk and then put his vest and shirt by it. His torso was lean and flat-muscled. The sheriff grunted at him again. "All right. That clears you. You can put your clothes on again." The sheriff turned toward the door.

"Wait just a minute, now," MacIver said. "What do you mean, clears me? What's this all about?"

The sheriff sighed, and spoke while MacIver was buttoning up his shirt. "A rider answering your description was one of the crowd that held up the stage this afternoon. He was wearing clothes exactly like the ones you have on. I talked to the livery stable hostler and he said you'd been out of town this afternoon. But there's one thing that clears you."

"And?"

"This fellow who looked like you—he's got a forty-five caliber hole through his shoulder. One of the guards on the stagecoach shot him at not more than fifteen feet range. He knows for sure exactly where he hit the man. He even saw the blood spurt. And you ain't got a hole in you, that's plain."

With that the sheriff swung heavily on his heel and left; and MacIver couldn't help bringing out a little smile of relief.

Then, before he had time to move, he saw the sheriff putting his head in the door again. "By the way, you would not just happen to know anything about a package that was left in the jail this afternoon, would you?"

"Package?" MacIver said. The sheriff turned away once again, shaking his head. MacIver smiled tightly, put on his gun and coat, and went out of the office, locking the door behind him. The sheriff was just leaving by the saloon's front door, not looking back. MacIver went as far as the near end of the bar, where he stopped and asked for a drink. The bartender delivered it and said, "I hear the sheriff recovered some of the money this time."

"That so? How much?"

"Three thousand dollars."

"Think of that," MacIver murmured. "Where'd he find it, Sandy?"

"He ain't sayin'."

MacIver nodded, glanced at the oil portrait of Marla, and lifted his drink.

V

STEPPING DOWN from the stagecoach in the heat of the midmorning sun, he was a medium-tall man with the thin flanks of a horseman and the flat gray stare of a gunfighter, and that was proper, for gunfighting was his trade; his name was Ethan Scott. But no one needed to ask his name. They knew him without asking. A sweeping black mustache guarded his wide lips and his deepset eyes were shadowed by thick black brows. His jaw had a slight jut to it and his hair, when he swept off his hat to wipe his forehead with a kerchief, was raven black, coming to a widow's peak atop his high brow. He would have been handsome except for his eyes. They were cold and impersonal and deadly as a snake's.

He wore a carefully cut frock coat swept back to reveal the black-rubber grips of a pair of shining Colt revolvers holstered low along his thighs. His costume was fawn-brown in color; his shoes were walking half-boots, without spurs. He wore a darker brown vest and a white shirt with string tie and again, had it not been for his guns and his eyes, he might have been taken for an itinerant gambler.

But he was not. He moved slowly, with a predator's suppleness and smoothness; he did not glare and he did not boast, and he threatened no one, except with the bleakness of his hollow gray eyes; yet he was, they said, the toughest man in Arizona.

He carried a single heavy carpetbag in his left hand. That was the extent of his luggage. He was the last passenger to step off the coach. Dropping to the ground, he paused to let his glance flick the pedestrians along the hotel porch; then he took his carpetbag up across the porch and into the high-ceilinged lobby. When he stopped at the desk the clerk did not ask his name; the clerk only said, "A room, sir?" And when Scott nodded, the clerk handed him a key. Scott glanced at the room number on the key. He turned his head, sweeping the faces peering in through the windows and doors, and carried his carpetbag upstairs.

That was the last the town saw of him for two hours, except for the lad who delivered buckets of steaming bath water to his room. But Ethan Scott did not have to be seen to be discussed. There was no other topic of conversation in the saloons and hotel lobbies and business offices, in the boardinghouses and stores and freightyards, and even in the cribs. Madam Yvette looked up with a stony glance and said in her whiskey-deep voice. "This town will rue the day—rue the day." And in the sheriff's office, Eugenio Castillo's portly shape paced up and down uncertainly. Down Bow Street in the office of the Hilltop Mining Company, Tom Larrabee walked in with his eyes brooding and said quietly, "Well, he's here."

And Guy Murvain nodded grimly. Larrabee said to him, "I think it's the greatest mistake you've ever made."

"Why, I thought you were in favor of it."

"Did you?" Larrabee's look was vague.

The news traveled up and down the street, a fire flamed by wind, carried on light gusts from lips to ears. Krayle MacIver heard it when he entered the Nugget at eleven o'clock. Ethan Scott had already been in Lodestar almost an hour, but all his life MacIver had been a late riser and so he did not learn the news till now. When Sandy, his head bartender, told him the word, his reaction was mixed. It would be good to see Scott again; but he feared for the town's future, for his own future. He remembered Careyville, and other towns, where the neatly dressed figure of Ethan Scott had stalked the streets, speaking with soft courtesy, taming the town with ruthless efficiency. He remembered those days well and it occurred to him that they always spelled the end for him and his kind; and so Krayle MacIver regretted this hour.

News of Scott's arrival did not penetrate far enough up into the Yellows to reach Henry Dierkes's ears until noontime, when Scott was already coming down the stairs into the lobby of the National Hotel.

A committee waited to welcome him.

MacIver stood back, not making his presence known immediately. Guy Murvain stepped forward from the body of men and spoke his own name, whereupon Ethan Scott nodded politely and shook Murvain's hand, his gray glance all the while sweeping the crowd.

From the back corner, in thickening shadows, MacIver watched all this before he stepped forward. He advanced toward Scott's flank, seeing Scott's head turn alertly; MacIver smiled and extended his hand. The almost imperceptible upturn at Scott's lip corners was a smile, though no one in the room but MacIver knew it. Scott gave him a quick, firm handshake and said, "So now it's Lodestar. You're doing well, Krayle."

"Yes." At this moment they stood several feet from the body of men and MacIver lowered his voice so that it reached no farther than Scott's ears. "I want to talk to you before you make any deals with these jackals."

Scott nodded, a slight dip of the head, and turned back to face Murvain and the rest of Murvain's crowd. Tom Larrabee and Sheriff Castillo both stepped forward, identifying themselves and shaking Scott's hand. Then Scott said, "Gentlemen?"

"Not here," Guy Murvain said quickly. He looked around. "We can talk in the dining room. Tom, I'll want you and the sheriff—and you can come too, MacIver."

"Much obliged," MacIver drawled.

"The rest of you wait for us," Murvain said brusquely, and moved his powerful frame through the wide opening to the dining room.

At this hour the room was empty. Murvain chose a big round table surrounded by half a dozen chairs and sat, putting his thick arms on the table and waiting with obvious impatience while the sheriff, Larrabee and MacIver took chairs around the table. Only then did Ethan Scott take a seat, and when he did it was in a chair that commanded the entire room.

Murvain opened the meeting. "Let's not waste time. I believe our telegram told you basically what we're up against here—and whatever it didn't say, you've probably picked up by hearsay along the trail."

Scott's eyes considered them, each in turn; MacIver felt the thrust of them. Scott said, "Sir, I only understand one thing at the moment. You gentlemen have offered to pay for my services."

"Exactly."

"I haven't learned yet what I'm to do, or what my capacity will be." At that moment Tom Larrabee's glance shifted to the sheriff, and lay there musingly. MacIver watched Ethan Scott carefully. The man didn't seem to have changed at all. MacIver had never in his life heard Scott raise his voice.

Murvain said, "I'm getting to that. It's been suggested—"

Scott cut him off sharply with two quiet words: "By whom?"

Murvain's head jerked up a fraction of an inch. "Members of the council and members of the mining combine."

"That's not good enough," Scott said. "Name them, please."

Murvain's glance sidled past MacIver to Sheriff Castillo, and then the sheriff's eyes grew hot with sudden realization; and Murvain said with some defensiveness in his tone, "By me. I suggested we have you appointed acting sheriff, Scott."

"You've already got a sheriff," Scott said, in a very conversational way.

"That can be taken care of." Murvain's tone was as dry as the whisper of wind in autumn-dry leaves.

Sheriff Castillo hadn't moved a muscle. Now he spoke without force. "I used to think I knew who my friends were."

"Friendship's one thing," Murvain said. "Survival's another. You're not doing the job, Gene—it's that simple."

Ethan Scott sat back. His hands never appeared from below the rim of the table. He said, "Go on, gentlemen."

The sheriff's big round face displayed no anger. He turned to look at Tom Larrabee, and Larrabee said, "I suggested that we hire you as a private agent of the mining combine."

Scott said nothing, and his silence seemed to make Guy Murvain think Scott needed more information. Murvain said, "The combine's a group of mine and reduction mill owners who've banded together for our mutual interest. You might compare us to a cattlemen's association."

"I gathered that much," Scott murmured. "I don't mean to sound blunt, but it would appear you're doing a lot of beating around the bush. Suggestions don't keep my stomach full. A motion made, seconded and passed—that's something else. But if you've just brought me here for speculation, I'm afraid we've both wasted our time."

Murvain's color deepened. "All right. Our problem is Henry Dierkes. Plain and simple—that's what you wanted, isn't it?"

The suggestion of a smile appeared once more at the edges of Scott's mouth. "It's a start."

"About being paid, I was about to add a minute ago that the combine has definitely decided to hire you as a private agent."

"Delightful," Scott breathed. MacIver heard the whispered word, but he doubted any of the others had caught it.

"Henry Dierkes," Murvain said heavily, "controls a loosely organized gang of toughs with headquarters up in the canyons of the Yellows. A lot of them are men who were run out of Tombstone. They're a hard lot and they've made it well nigh impossible for any of us to run profitable mining operations here. They've attacked payroll shipments and high-graded ore wagons in broad daylight and jumped claims belonging to small independents. As a pastime they rustle cattle in Mexico and sell them here, and rustle stock here and sell it in Mexico. Yesterday they robbed an Overland stagecoach that was carrying a twenty-eight-thousand dollar payroll belonging to the Hilltop Mining Company. I happen to own Hilltop, and I'm expecting a cancellation notice any day now from the outfit that covers my payrolls with insurance. And even if they don't cancel immediately, I'm still losing money, because insurance won't cover the whole of any loss over five thousand dollars. And since I haven't been able to get a payroll delivered in damn near three months, some of my men have already quit and most of the rest are ready to quit. The rest of the mine owners are in the same hole. Larrabee here owns Lodgepole, which is the second biggest in tonnage, and his problems are exactly the same as mine."

"I see," Ethan Scott said. "And you blame Henry Dierkes for all your losses."

MacIver caught the sheriff's soft chuckle, and the quick angry glance that Murvain slapped against the sheriff. Ethan Scott looked at the sheriff and said, "Have you any proof against Dierkes?"

"Nothing that would hold up in court." The sheriff moved uncomfortably under Scott's flat gaze.

"Which makes the law powerless," Scott observed.

"That's it," the sheriff said. "My hands are tied. That's what I've been trying to tell them."

Scott's lips moved slightly. "I'm sure you have."

"Then it's settled," Murvain said, laying his palms flat on the table, ready to rise. "You'll work for the combine."

"Perhaps," Scott said. His single mild word fell among them deadly flat; it brought a stillness of astonishment to the small group—and Murvain said, "What's that?"

"You haven't hired me yet, and I haven't agreed to take the job. What am I offered?"

Scott's glance was bitter cold. Murvain said, "A thousand a month, and a ten-thousand-dollar bonus if and when you eliminate the problems caused by Dierkes and his crew."

"Eliminate the problems," Scott said, and added, "That takes in a lot of territory."

"It also gives you plenty of leeway," Murvain said, slightly angered. "You'll have a free hand to operate in any way you choose."

"As long as I remain within the law."

"I didn't say that," Murvain said quickly.

"No. I observed you didn't. I said it. That's the way I work, sir—within the letter of the law."

Murvain shrugged, a bit suggestively. "You made that rule. I didn't."

Scott dipped his head in courteous acquiescence. "I wanted to make myself clear. Perhaps you'll want to change your mind about hiring me."

"No," Murvain said.

Tom Larrabee's eyes were sleepy-lidded, but his voice was sharp with intensity. "Damn it, man, we don't care how you get the job done. Just do it."

Our pious leading citizens, MacIver thought. Guy Murvain said, "Then it's settled," for the second time. "You're on the payroll as of now."

"Not quite. I still haven't accepted your offer."

Murvain stiffened. "What?"

"I'll consider it," Scott said smoothly. "Suppose I meet you tomorrow and give you my answer?"

Murvain blinked. "Why, for a two-bit tough you've sure got your gall, Scott!"

"You're bullying the wrong man," Scott said, unruffled. "You can withdraw the offer if you wish."

Murvain swore a muffled oath. He stood up, knocking his chair back, wheeled and left the room without speaking again. It was indication enough that the meeting was ended. Larrabee watched Murvain disappear; a tight little smile played on Larrabee's lips and he said, "Guy's going to bite off a mouthful of trouble one day."

That could apply just as well to you, my friend, MacIver thought. Larrabee and the sheriff left soon afterward, leaving MacIver alone in the big dining room with Scott. MacIver stood up and said: "The lunch crowd will be in here shortly. We can talk in my office."

Scott nodded and stepped along beside him. "How've you been, Krayle?"

"So-so," MacIver muttered, and led the way to the street. He noted the stares of the curious and the awe-filled on all sides; he noted the glitter of Ethan Scott's eyes, absorbing every detail into the perceptive mind. Scott's hands swung in short, smooth arcs, brushing the handles of his black-gripped guns with every step. They turned into the Nugget and Scott paused, accustoming his eyes to the relative dimness of the place, looking around without visible expression. "This is yours," he said.

"Yes."

"Big," was Scott's muttered observation. MacIver smiled a small smile in answer to Scott's dry understatement, and led Scott to the door of his office, which he unlocked and swung open. Then he stepped back and lifted his arm in a gesture.

"Go ahead," Scott said.

MacIver's face darkened slightly but he went on into the office, waiting to close the door after Scott. Then he put the key in the lock and locked the door and went around his desk. "You don't trust me, then."

"I trust no one. You'll forgive me—it's hard to break a habit."

"Maybe," MacIver said. He peeled back the lapel of his coat to show the short-barreled gun in his shoulder holster. "I'm going to take it out and put it on top of the safe."

"What for?"

"Maybe you'll be a little more comfortable," MacIver said. "I never saw you loosen up as much as an inch as long as you were in a room with an armed man."

"All right," Scott said mildly. "Suit yourself."

MacIver set his gun on the safe and walked back of the desk to sit down. He put his feet up on the desk's corner and extracted a pair of slim cheroots from his vest pocket, one of which he tossed toward Scott. Scott's hand flicked up and caught the cigar in mid-flight; he put it between his lips and spat out the tip and found a match. "Thanks."

"*De nada*. Sit down."

Scott pushed a chair back beside the door and lowered himself into it. "Been almost four years, hasn't it?"

"Just about." MacIver's tone was muffled because he was puffing on his own cheroot to get it going. When it was smoking to his satisfaction he slid the window open and sat back, tossing his broken match into the spittoon by the desk corner. "You make bigger tracks all the time, Ethan."

Scott's eyes reflected frostily. "Do I?"

MacIver smiled. "I didn't mean to rub a sore spot. Forget it. I trust *you*, Ethan."

"That's fine," Scott murmured. "You can afford to." But he showed no sign of relaxing his guard.

"I remember once you had a shooting match with a bird who calls himself Raven."

"I winged him," Scott said, and smiled a little.

MacIver nodded. "He works for Henry Dierkes now. His number three man. I thought you ought to know."

"I'm obliged."

"That's a pretty hard bunch riding with Dierkes."

"How does he control them?"

"He doesn't, most of the time. He doesn't try. That's why he's boss up there. He keeps a few men around him who are willing to take orders. Raven's one of those."

"Who are the others?"

"A young Mex who's quick with his knife, and a heavyset fellow named Arnie. Arnie's good with his fists and good with his gun. You know Dierkes, don't you?"

"We shared a cellblock in Yuma," Scott said in his customary dry, quiet way. "He's a friendly sort."

"And tough."

"Yes."

"The rest of the crew is a wild bunch, independent gentlemen of the trail."

"I know the kind," Scott said. "They take orders from no one, but when Dierkes shows them an opportunity for a big take they'll be willing enough to organize temporarily. And between jobs he gives them shelter and provisions."

"Exactly. They make their headquarters up in a series of abandoned prospecting camps in the Yellows. The Yellows are as rugged as the trail to Hell."

Scott nodded and studied the gentle rise of smoke from the gray tip of his cigar. "The sheriff said he has no proof against Dierkes. What do you think?"

"I think Dierkes runs the toughs, and the toughs pull the holdups. But somebody's behind Dierkes."

"Who?"

Preserve the legacy of the Old West in distinctive hardcover volumes...

THE LOUIS L'AMOUR COLLECTIO

Now you and your family can experience the authentic Old West...its rich lore and legend in a rugged, handsome series: The Louis L'Amour Collection—superb hardcover Heritage Editions, meticulously bound in padded Sierra-brown leatherette.

Each matching volume— with the look and feel of hand-rubbed saddle leather—is an enduring testament to our unique American past...a tribute to the narrative power of Louis L'Amour, the most popular writer of frontier adventures who ever lived.

Start your Louis L'Amour Collection now with FLINT—a gripping novel of murder and revenge—FREE for 10 days. If you decide to keep it, further volumes may be previewed each month, also for 10 days free. Each volume contributes to an impressive home library, certain to become a treasured family heirloom...to be enjoyed again and again.

Mail the card at right today.

Now in handsome Heritage Editions

Each matching 6" x 9" volume in The Collection is bound in rich Sierra-brown leatherette, with padded covers and embossed gold title... creating an enduring family library of distinction.

"I don't know," MacIver admitted. "But I've got access to a good number of grapevines, and the smell's there all right. Between that and a few stray facts I've picked up myself, I've become pretty certain somebody's backing Henry's play—somebody with good reason."

"Somebody like yourself, perhaps," Scott said without tone.

MacIver smiled. "Possible."

"But not true."

"No. For a while I was almost certain it was Tom Larrabee. Larrabee's young and tough and ambitious and it doesn't trouble him to step on people. Ask him and he'll admit it. But now I'm not sure of him."

"Why?"

"Yesterday," MacIver said, "I made the mistake of jumping to a conclusion about Larrabee. I found out I was wrong."

He leaned forward, elbows on the desk, and told Scott of the attempted frame-up against him yesterday afternoon. He told of the stage robbery and showed Scott the anonymous note that had tolled him out of town, and told of finding the money in his safe and of later confronting Tom Larrabee with his accusation. When he was finished he found his cigar had grown a tall ash, and he reached out to the spittoon to tap it off. Then he said, "Larrabee was right about one thing. I've got a tendency to be a little careless about my valuables. So I'm not so sure about him any more. It could be Murvain, it could be one of the other mineowners or even a businessman in town. It might even be the sheriff."

"I doubt that," Scott said. "After a look at him, I doubt it."

"Sometimes looks are deceptive."

Scott exhaled a ball of smoke. "I trust my instincts, my hunches. It's a good way to stay alive. I wouldn't be surprised to find your sheriff tied up with Dierkes, but he's not the man behind Dierkes. He hasn't the guts or the intelligence, and he probably hasn't got the money."

"What do you mean? Money?"

"What would a man stand to gain by backing Henry Dierkes's raids?"

"Those payrolls aren't inconsequential," MacIver said.

Scott shook his head in disagreement. "How many men does Dierkes have?"

MacIver thought about it. "That's questionable. It varies—his men come and go. Somewhere between forty and seventy, I'd say."

"Well, then, assume it's fifty. Now, what would you say the losses to thievery have amounted to over the past year?"

"Maybe a hundred and fifty thousand dollars, maybe more. I can't say."

"Three thousand dollars per man," Scott muttered. "Not much, is it? And then you've got to figure that Dierkes is probably taking more than an equal share. On an average, maybe each man gets two thousand dollars. That's no fortune for a year's thieving."

MacIver frowned. "Now that you mention it, it isn't."

"Those toughs are working pretty cheap," Scott said. "And you can be sure if there's a man behind Dierkes, that man isn't cutting himself in for much of the take. He's got some other motive than that."

"What, then?"

"Suppose you owned a mine on the slope and you got greedy. Suppose you weren't satisfied with your own slice of the pie. Suppose you wanted the whole pie. What would you do?"

"I'm not that greedy," MacIver said. "I'm satisfied with a fair wedge of pie."

"What if you weren't? What if you wanted control of the whole slope?"

"There's no easy way," MacIver argued. "Why, to get the whole silver lode, a man would have to drive all the other companies off the slope, and keep them off."

"Exactly," Scott murmured, and let the echo of his quiet word ring in the room.

And then it hit MacIver, and he sat back as though a fist had been rammed into his chest. "Drive them all out of business," he breathed. "Sure. I'll be damned."

"Perhaps we all will," Scott said with that slightest of smiles characteristic of him. "But the fact remains that the easiest way to drive the mines out of business is to keep

Dierkes robbing them blind until they're forced to close up. A man wealthy enough to weather through would be in a good position to step in. He can't afford not to be robbed right now, along with the others, or he'd be caught."

"It's all a theory," MacIver said cautiously. "But it could be true, couldn't it? Think of that."

Scott nodded. "I intend to."

"Then you'll take the job?"

Scott watched him levelly. "Earlier, you said you wanted to talk to me before I accepted Murvain's offer. Why?"

MacIver shrugged. "Personal reasons. I've seen what happens to towns like this when the people get the law-and-order bug crawling around in their insides."

"So have I. In the end they'll always turn against you and me and men like us."

MacIver nodded. "And when they pull us down, we're all through. We're on the wrong side of the street, Ethan. I like the town the way it is—I don't want change. That's why I'm reluctant to see you take this job."

Scott's shoulders lifted slightly, settled and dropped. "It will change with or without me."

"It would take a good deal longer, without you."

"Perhaps. It might be wise for you to sell out while you can still make a profit."

"It would be wise," MacIver agreed. "But I'm enough of a fool to want to watch the fun."

"You did that in Careyville too, I remember."

"Did I?" MacIver said distantly. "Well, I came out of it all right, and it was fun. I wouldn't want to have missed it." He smiled.

"Sometimes," Scott said, "I suspect you're the same as the rest of them, Krayle—a vulture just sitting around, eager for the day when somebody cuts Ethan Scott down and scatters the pieces on the street."

MacIver shook his head. "I'm no vulture. I'm a friend of yours, though most of the time I don't think you know it. I don't wait to see you killed—but you and I both know it will happen one day. It's a part of the life you lead. You can't avoid it. But I'm not hungry to see it. I hope I never do."

"Then why stay?"

"I always hope to see the vultures caught in their own trap," MacIver said in a faraway manner. "I haven't seen it yet, but one day I hope to. The ones like Murvain—pompous and pious and arrogant and self-righteous to Hell and gone. They always seem to wind up at the top of the heap, but I'm still waiting for the day when the heap crumbles and spills them down to the bottom with the rest of us. It's worth waiting for."

"Don't count on it. It never happens that way."

"Then what makes you live the way you do?"

Scott's shoulders moved slightly. He said in hollow echo, "Hard to say. Circumstances, experience—habit, I guess. Can you explain your life? We push ourselves into corners we can't get out of. I just keep shooting at the wall, trying to break it down. But I never will."

"No, I don't think you will." MacIver crammed his cheroot out in the spittoon. "Why don't you quit?"

"I can't." Scott stood up, turning to the door. "I'll see you later."

MacIver nodded silently. As soon as Scott was gone, he stood up and went as far as the door, intending to push it shut. But then something he saw up front in the saloon arrested him and he stood with one hand resting gently against the doorjamb. Half obscured by the thickness of the crowd, Ethan Scott had paused near the door to speak with someone. That was Marla Searles. After a moment Scott tipped his hat courteously and went outside to the boardwalk, and MacIver's glance rose to rest on the portrait of Marla that hung provocatively over the back bar mirror.

It was three o'clock before MacIver realized he had eaten no lunch today, an observation that surprised him because he was normally a man of exact habit. Hunger made itself plain and he moved his bantam figure down Bow Street past Third and Fourth to Nita Matlock's café, and turned in out of the bitterly lashing sun. Dust coated his boots and his clothes. Except for himself and Nita, no one was in the café. He took his usual place at the counter and when Nita looked at him she said, "You're late today."

"I know. I can't quite account for it."

"You're not usually forgetful," she said, smiling her smile of polite friendliness.

It made him study her more carefully than he had before. She was a tall girl with a good slim figure, round and firm with strength. She was, perhaps, twenty-seven or twenty-eight. Her hair and eyes were black—the hair as black as Ethan Scott's. MacIver said, "I suppose I'll have my usual."

"Not getting tired of it?"

"Maybe I am," he said.

"Why not try ribs today?"

He thought about it. "I believe I might. All right, I'll try the ribs." For some reason it gave him a good feeling. He looked up at her and said, "Yes."

Her smile was, he thought, more friendly than usual; he said, "You know, a man wonders why a girl like you isn't married."

"I was," she said.

"Oh. I'm sorry."

"Don't be," she said. "It was a long time ago. My husband is dead—killed in Tombstone."

"Tombstone," he said, and smiled vaguely. "You must have spent a good part of your life in mining camps, then."

"Yes."

He nodded. "I'll have those ribs," he said positively. The girl went back into the kitchen and MacIver leaned against the counter, silent with his thoughts over the stretching interval of time. Light traffic passed by on the street outside. He thought of Ethan Scott and he felt an abstract sadness, a reluctance to see himself regurgitated by the town he had probably helped build—but he knew it would come to pass, probably quickly. And it was the thought of the town changing, as much as his own personal impending loss, that troubled him. Never again would the town own vitality anything like what it owned now. The raw, open passions of men would be curbed when the vultures took over, pacifying the town with their leaden good intentions. Exhilaration and violence would disappear from the face of the land. This was one of the last of the frontiers and he was made unhappy to know it was dying.

When Nita returned with his lunch he picked up his fork and then hesitated, turning his glance on her. She stood behind the counter idly wiping clean dishes with a corner of her apron. MacIver said, "My father was a barber, a Scotsman. He always wanted me to be a barber."

"A lot of us never become what we want to become," she said.

"I've got no complaints. Have you?"

"I don't know," she said, quite seriously. "It's a drab shop, you know."

Something occurred to MacIver then, something he had heard Tom Larrabee say to Nita the other night, and he said, "Today's Friday, isn't it?"

"Yes."

"I understand a traveling troupe's putting on a show at the theater tomorrow night. I'm wondering what you meant when you turned Larrabee down. Would you go to the theater with me?"

Her head cocked to one side while she considered him. MacIver removed his hat and put it on the counter, revealing his smooth head of silver hair. Presently the girl nodded. "All right," she said.

VI

FROM THE corner-fronting doorway of the Nugget, facing the sun in the late afternoon, MacIver watched Tom Larrabee cross the street down below and walk into the offices of the Crystal Freight Company, apparently on a business errand. Ambitious energy seemed to be driving Larrabee willfully, and once again MacIver wondered if Larrabee had any part in Henry Dierkes's activities. Then MacIver's head swivelled to look up Bow Street, and he saw a familiar figure advancing—Ethan Scott, walking

down from the hotel with a strange, brisk deliberation.
Something was on Scott's mind. No one else would have
seen that, but MacIver knew Scott as well as any man
alive could know the withdrawn fighting man. Scott's strict
reserve was always held by close guard, but there were
little surface signs that gave his feelings away to a man who
knew him. Having been a professional gambler most of his
life, MacIver was keenly alert to these tiny signals.

Somewhere in the run of these few moments MacIver
felt the touch of intimations of trouble. It was in the way
Scott walked, in the way he had held his head, in the way
his long-muscled shoulders rolled as he moved down the
street, cruising with supple grace. MacIver's spirit whirled
up half-apprehensively. Half a block away, Scott dropped
off the walk and came forward through the dust of Bow
Street, quartering across toward the point where MacIver
stood in front of the Nugget. And when Scott arrived on
the walk, MacIver said to him, "You took the job."

"Yes."

"Just now?"

"Quite a while ago—a few hours."

"Then what's spooking you?"

Scott's glance flicked him frostily. "Am I spooked?"

"Not to anybody else. To me you are."

"All right," Scott said, "something's come up."

"And?"

"Let's go inside," Scott said. His hollow glance swept
the street in both directions. MacIver curbed his tongue
and went inside the Nugget. Trade was light at this hour.
A few cowboys and perhaps a dozen miners rattled around
loosely in the place. MacIver led the way back to his
office, shut the door behind Scott and turned. "What is
it?"

"Word just came down. Henry Dierkes is on his way."

"Here?"

Scott nodded. "He's got two or three men with him,
perhaps more."

"I see," MacIver said. "Then he intends to call your
bluff."

"He intends to try," Scott said softly. "But what was
on my mind is this. When he comes, he'll head here first.

I understand he generally uses this place as his headquarters when he comes to town."

"Now and then. Henry seems to feel that the best the town has to offer is none too good for him. And the Nugget's the best in town, according to his way of thinking."

Scott's faint suggestion of a smile appeared. "What about your way of thinking?"

MacIver shrugged. "I'm on the wrong side of the town. But it's a place to do business. How soon do you expect Dierkes?"

"Within a half hour."

"How'd you find out they were coming?"

"The first thing a man does in my position," Scott told him, "is to organize his own grapevine."

"Fast work," MacIver observed.

"Fast or dead. It's that way in my line."

"Yeah," MacIver breathed softly. "I guess it is. Thanks for the warning, Ethan."

Scott nodded. "If you don't mind I'll wait for them out front."

"Try not to smash up the place," MacIver said drily.

"I'll try," Scott said, matching his tone for dryness, and left the office.

MacIver went around his desk and was about to sit down when he noticed that his revolver was still lying on top of the safe where he had put it that morning during his first talk with Scott. He grunted with irritation and went to the safe, picking the gun up and shoving it into its scabbard under his coat. *Someday,* he thought, *your damned carelessness is going to bring you grief, MacIver*. With the weight of the gun hugging his chest he returned to his chair and sat.

He glanced at his watch, and put it away in its pocket. It was a few minutes past six o'clock. Dierkes and his crew would arrive in about a half hour—six-thirty. It was a good four-hour ride down from the part of the Yellows where most of Dierkes's toughs stayed. That meant they must have left the mountain stronghold at about two-thirty. If a man had ridden out of Lodestar, intending to warn Dierkes, that man would have had to leave Lodestar no later than ten-thirty this morning—just about the time Ethan Scott had stepped off the stagecoach, arriving in town. That meant whoever had ridden up to warn Dierkes had not waited to find out whether Scott was going to take the job offered him by the combine. He must have ridden out of town as soon as he had seen Scott. That meant whoever had sent the warning to Dierkes had been pretty sure all along that Scott would take the job.

And it had been Murvain, not Larrabee, who had been so all-fired certain Scott would accept the combine's offer. Yesterday Larrabee had expressed doubts that Scott would want any part of the odds presented by Dierkes and his army of rawhiders. All of which led MacIver to wonder if it wasn't Murvain after all, instead of Larrabee, who was the force behind Henry Dierkes.

But it was all conjecture, nothing more. MacIver got up and went forward into the saloon, noticing right away that Ethan Scott had posted himself at a table halfway along the Bow Street side of the room with his back to the wall and his hands out of sight under the rim of the table. Scott's chair was tipped back and he seemed indolent and idle as any man alive; but his eyes glittered brightly. MacIver nodded to him and went to the near end of the bar, where he asked for a drink and put his eye on the crowd restlessly. It wasn't a big crowd, but it was a shaky one—everyone in the room knew who Ethan Scott was, and most of them suspected why he was here. They were ready to bolt, MacIver could see. Out front, the water wagon rattled by the front door, sprinkling the street to keep the dust dampened down.

When MacIver's head barkeep, Sandy, came down to his end of the bar, MacIver called him over. "Let one of the relief bartenders take over for you. Post yourself in the lookout box with the shotgun."

"Expect trouble?"

"Maybe. That's Ethan Scott sitting over there, and in a few minutes Henry Dierkes and his boys will be walking in the front door. You figure it out."

Sandy's jaw clamped tight. "Yeah," he said, and moved away, untying his apron. A few minutes later MacIver saw him in the lookout pulpit with the butt end of the short-barreled shotgun visible behind his elbow. From across the room MacIver caught Ethan Scott's small nod. Scott took off his hat and placed it carefully on the table in front of him. His chair dropped forward to stand square on all four legs and Scott leaned forward, lifting one hand above the table's edge. A gun glistened momentarily and then Scott's hand was hidden under the hat. Scott's head turned; lamplight raced off the sheen of his black hair. He was watching the door intently but without visible anxiety.

MacIver turned and walked back to the far corner of the saloon where the piano stood on a small two-foot-high dais. The professor sat by the piano with a drink in his hand. "Take a break," MacIver said, and the professor went away spryly after a single glance at Ethan Scott. To command the room and make a triangle of fire with Scott and Sandy, if necessary, MacIver climbed upon the dais and idly rested his elbow against the lid of the upright piano, so that his hand lay across his chest against his coat. He caught the touch of a look from Scott and he thought he saw Scott shake his head back and forth very slightly. Scott probably wanted him to stay out of this. *What the Hell*, MacIver thought—*it's my saloon, isn't it?* His hand flicked back the lapel of his coat and slid to a point only an inch from the butt of his concealed gun; and he stood that way, his eyes fixed on the door, while his ears caught the swell and rush of advancing hoofbeats and then, looking across the intersection through the doors, he saw a crowd of horsemen drumming forward. *Right on time*, he thought.

They wheeled to a halt, the riders, lifting a high turbulence of dust. A rapid tally counted five or six of them. They had gone out of sight beyond the door but MacIver knew they would be tying up their horses at the hitch rails on Bow Street. They would be around to the door in a minute.

It surprised him to see that it was not Henry Dierkes who led the toughs into the Nugget. It was the Mex who pushed through the batwing doors and walked straight toward the bar, not even glancing toward Scott sitting along the far wall. But MacIver would have bet his life the Mex had spotted Ethan and knew Ethan's exact position every minute. The Mex continued forward past the thin scatter of customers and advanced the whole length of

he bar, coming close to MacIver's position before stopping
t the end of the bar. The Mex coolly put his back to
MacIver, leaning an elbow against the wood and tipping
his hat back off his forehead, which allowed a lick of oily
black hair to flop down.

Not until then did the others enter. They came in a
pack, four of them, and still MacIver did not see Henry
Dierkes. Dierkes must be playing it safe, setting up his
play before walking into it. Of the four men now coming
forward, MacIver recognized two: Arnie, the heavyset
brawler, and Raven, the Texas killer, gaunt and malicious.
The other two were run-of-the-mill hairpins, bearded and
dirty-clothed. These four spread out at equal intervals
along the bar, all of them patently ignoring Ethan Scott by
putting their backs to him and leaning against the bar. But
MacIver knew, and so did Scott, that everything that went
on in the saloon was visible to those men in the backbar
mirrors. *So far*, MacIver observed, *it's all strictly according to the pattern. An old game—will it never end?*

Raven, the gaunt gunman, moved away from the bar
carrying his drink and ambled with an all-too-obvious
aimlessness to a table near the door of MacIver's office.
This put Raven far to Scott's left; the door was to Scott's
right. It made a neat crossfire, MacIver thought, and he
turned to put his attention flatly on Raven, considering
Raven to be the most dangerous man in the place. He
trusted Sandy to cover the men along the bar with his
shotgun when the trouble started. MacIver knew for a
certainty that trouble would start. Watching Raven, he saw
the gaunt man hunch his shoulders and bend over, coughing
into his cupped hand; and when Raven's spasm was ended,
he took his hand away from his lips and his hand was
covered with blood.

Not until then did Henry Dierkes make his entrance.
He appeared at the door and wandered idly through it and
stepped aside to put his back to the wall beside the door.
He said nothing and looked at no one in particular. But the
patrons of the saloon didn't need any warning beyond
Dierkes's presence. Talk stopped like an abrupt intake of
breath. Men milled out from the bar and headed for the

door in a stream. Not until the last straggler was gone did Henry Dierkes move.

Dierkes looked back at MacIver across sixty feet of hardwood floor and grinned his friendly, cheerful grin, after which he stepped forward precisely five paces. Tall, flat-stomached and lean, he stood with unhurried ease. His legs were spread two feet at the boots; his knees were a trifle bent; his weight was thrown slightly forward, as if in anticipation. Even from this distance MacIver could distinguish the freckles on Dierkes's skin. Then MacIver returned his attention to Raven and kept it there, moving his hand across his chest a few inches to grasp the butt of his gun. Raven ignored him; Raven's eyes were on Henry Dierkes, and MacIver assumed Raven was awaiting a signal.

No one had spoken; all this had taken place without the need for directions. Each man who was a part of it had seen the same scene take shape many times before; no one needed telling. Ethan Scott sat motionless at his table, his hand under his hat, his face drawn down in weary lines. His cold eyes regarded Dierkes bleakly. "Hello, Henry."

"Long time no see," Dierkes said. His voice cut forward strongly, cheerfully across the dead silence.

"Aye," Scott murmured.

"I expect that's a gun you're hidin' under your hat," Dierkes said.

"It might be."

"You think that's fair?"

"I count six of you," Scott said. "If you intend it, you may as well get down to business, Henry."

Dierkes stood silent a moment; a sort of puzzlement crossed his face and his eyes remained on the hat covering Scott's hand. He said, "I only came to make somethin' clear. A lot of people have made loose remarks about me and my boys, but nobody's proved a thing against us."

"Then you don't have much to fret about, do you?" Scott's tone was uncompromising but not bullying. MacIver watched Raven's thin blue-veined hands intently.

"All right," Henry Dierkes said abruptly, and then did a strange thing: he turned with a quick snap of his high shoulders and walked out the door. The slap of his bootheels against the boardwalk echoed back and was absorbed into silence. MacIver could not conceal his surprise. Why had Dierkes backed down? He heard Raven's rasping cough and Raven's bitter words: "The yellow bastard!"

It was in that moment, while MacIver was taken aback by Dierkes's startling departure from the saloon, that the move came. It was Raven who started the ball, Raven whose hand dipped silently below the table behind which he sat; and on that signal MacIver whipped out his gun and trained it instantly on the man. "Hold it, Raven."

Raven froze; but it was too late. Along the bar, four men were swinging around, three of them reaching for the guns at their belts and the fourth, the Mex, flicking up his knife. Light raced fragmentarily along the blade of the long knife and then MacIver heard the double-throated roar of Sandy's eight-gauge shotgun. The buckshot took the Mex square in the belly and slammed him back against the bar hard enough to rock every glass on its surface; and then the swell and pound of gunfire distracted MacIver and he remembered, in time, to whip his attention back to Raven.

But Raven hadn't stirred. He only sat watching MacIver unwinkingly. Sixguns talked in harsh signals throughout the huge room; powder smoke was acrid in his nostrils and burned his eyes. Several lamps went out from concussion. Someone fell with a loud thud; the room was plunged into a twilight dimness; there was a brief, ragged aftervolley of shots and then the room was still.

Outside MacIver heard the lift of many voices. He did not take his eyes off Raven. He walked forward with his gun steady and paused when he stood by Raven. Behind him nothing stirred. He pushed the table away and lifted the guns from Raven's holsters and tossed them away. Raven said, "Never fight the drop. But I'll remember this, MacIver. No man alive can get away with this—you ain't tough enough, bucko."

"We'll see," MacIver answered.

The Mex was sprawled face down at the base of the bar, one arm hooked over the brass rail. The shotgun blast had cut him in two. His blood stained the floor.

Closer up by the end of the bar, the heavy-set tough Arnie stood clutching a wounded arm. Nearer the door one man was down, plainly dead, and the other stood unharmed with his arms up, trying to scratch the high ceiling.

And Ethan Scott—Ethan Scott sat at the table just the way he had been before it all started, except for his two hands, which rested on top of the table now, both of them gripping short-barreled Colt revolvers. Scott's hat lay on the floor beside him where he must have tossed it. He talked to the man at the front of the room, the one with his hands up. "Drag your friends out of here."

Scott's voice was no different in tone that it had been at any time today. Smoke drifted quietly from the muzzles of his guns. His eyes were half-lidded. He put down one of his revolvers and lifted his hand to twist the points of his mustache while the unarmed tough went back and hoisted his dead companion over his shoulders and walked forward under that load, out of the saloon.

That left the dead Mex and the wounded Arnie, and Raven, who sat in a chair, with the table thrown aside, bent over and coughing. Sandy, the bartender, broke open his shotgun and inserted two fresh shells. Then he snapped the shotgun closed, cocked the twin hammers and swung to command Raven with the gun. "Pick up the Mex and drift."

Raven stood up, making no quick motions. His dismal, hateful glance traveled from MacIver to Sandy to Ethan Scott, and rested on Scott for a stretching moment. Then Raven moved to the bar and stooped, grunting, to pick up the Mexican kid. Blood splashed over Raven's clothes. He coughed consumptively and staggered forward under the Mex's weight. MacIver looked at Arnie and said flatly, "You too."

Clutching his wounded arm, Arnie walked to the door and disappeared after Raven.

All the breath that had collected in MacIver's chest was released in a long sigh. He pushed his unfired gun back into its holster under his arm, and walked unsteadily to the bar. "Pour us all a drink, Sandy. A tall one."

"Reckon it wouldn't be out of place," Sandy said, in not too certain a tone. He uncocked the shotgun and put it away, and went around behind the bar. MacIver hooked his elbows over the bar, with his back to it, and let his glance ride across the room toward Scott. Scott stood up slowly, holstered his guns and stopped to pick up his hat. Then he came forward and stood against the bar beside MacIver. MacIver said, "You're the only man I ever knew with nerve enough not to jump out of his seat at a time like that."

"No point in jumping," Scott said. "You can't dodge a bullet. Krayle, you shouldn't have mixed in this. Now Dierkes and Raven will have it in for you—and you're no gunman."

"That may be," MacIver said. "But I had to do it, didn't I?"

"Why?"

"What's a friend for?"

Scott's answering glance chilled him all the way down to his heels. "I have no friends," Scott whispered, and walked away toward the door.

God, MacIver thought dismally. Out front the crowd was swelling forward; he turned to face them.

VII

DIERKES HAD LAID down his challenge and Ethan Scott had accepted it. The town now waited to see what would develop next. Like scavengers they waited; they had smelled gunsmoke now; they had tasted blood—and they expected more. Scott had won the first round but no one was fool enough to think the matter settled. And now the scavengers prowled up the streets and they would be unsatisfied until the job was done completely.

Eugenio Castillo was afraid and he did not mind admitting it to himself. He admitted it to others, too: in particular, to Henry Dierkes. He sat on the tiny stoop of Dierkes's sagging cabin, tilting his hat against the cool wind, with the midnight moon washing his face with a pale yellow lacquer. He said, "I don't like it."

"Don't worry about it," Dierkes said mildly.

The sheriff pulled a red bandanna out of his hip pocket and smoothed it out. He took off his hat to use the bandanna to mop moisture—the oil-sweat of nerves—from his face. "It wasn't like you to leave the boys in there to face him alone," he said.

"I'm no coward," Dierkes said to him. "Don't ever make that mistake."

"No."

"But I ain't a fool either. And now I live to fight another day—you see? I've known Ethan Scott a good long time, long enough to know he takes a lot of lickin'. But don't you forget this: he's the only man alive I'll make that remark about."

The sheriff nodded silently, and behind him, Raven moved his gaunt shape out of the cabin, knocking his bony knee into the sheriff's fleshy back when he went past. Raven went down into the yard, paused and looked back over his shoulder. "Hell, he ain't so tough. One man—one bullet. That's all it takes."

"Sure," Henry Dierkes said quietly. "Maybe you'll get the chance, Raven."

"I've been itchin' for it ever since he put a bullet in my arm in Tombstone. Listen, if it hadn't been for that runt saloonkeeper yesterday—"

"I know," Dierkes said. "I know. You'll get another try at him."

"I'm countin' on it," Raven said. He coughed and went on toward the barn. Back in the cabin, behind the sheriff, a voice came weakly through the open door—the voice of the wounded Arnie. "Somebody gimme some whiskey."

Dierkes stood up, a little irritated. "All right. Keep your pants on, Arnie. Judas, if I had just one man I could depend on..." His voice trailed off and he went petulantly into the cabin. The sheriff heard the gurgle of liquid pouring from bottle to glass and then Arnie's hoarse "Thanks." Dierkes came back outside, shutting the door behind him, and sat down beside the sherrif on the stoop. His face was more dour than usual; he displayed none of his customary devil-may-care cheer.

"Raven talks tough," the sheriff said, "but he can't whip Ethan Scott."

"No," Dierkes said, "I doubt he can. Scott's a hell of a man, Gene."

The sheriff nodded; and Dierkes said, "You know, there's only one thing that's kept Ethan Scott from becoming top dog in this territory."

The sheriff turned his head to look at Dierkes. "To look at the way people walk around him on tiptoe, you'd think he *was* top dog."

Dierkes shook his head. "They're scared of him, but they don't respect him."

"They respect his gun."

"If you want to call that respect." Dierkes spun up a cigarette and snapped his thumbnail over the head of a match to light it. He said, "Scott's one of the shrewdest men I've ever met. He's got brains and he's got charm, when he wants to use it. I said he could be top dog—and he could, too, except for one thing."

"What thing?"

"Pride," Dierkes murmured. "Gun pride. He's got to keep provin' over and over again that he's the toughest man in Arizona. If it wasn't for that, he'd be bigger than Murvain and Larrabee and all your damned big boys. But he's too proud—and his pride makes him scared to take off his guns."

The sheriff shook his head back and forth, not quite understanding Dierkes's meaning, not agreeing with what he did understand of it. And when Dierkes looked at him, Dierkes seemed to recognize that his talk was going over the sheriff's head, for he said, "What about that payroll for the Mountain King mine?"

"Monday afternoon," the sheriff said. "They're trying the stagecoach again. There's a rumor Scott will be riding shotgun on the stage."

Dierkes's glance remained troubled, but he said, "Raven will like that." He sounded a little sour. His face moved; he regarded the sheriff directly. "It might be a good idea for you to ride that stagecoach too."

"Me?"

"Sure," Dierkes said. "When it gets held up you can do some shootin'. Just make sure you don't hit anybody."

"I don't get it," the sheriff said. "You want me to ride the coach—what for?"

"To make it look good. I want you to stay in office, Gene. This way you'll avoid suspicion."

"All right," the sheriff said grudgingly. "But up on that box with Scott I'd feel like a magnet to draw every bullet."

"Then ride inside. You won't get hurt."

"You ever seen the way Raven looks at me? He's just itching for a chance to gun me down and call it an accident."

"Raven won't bother you," Dierkes said. His tone was gentle but firm.

"It's easy for you to talk. You won't be on that stage."

Dierkes's head cocked over; he considered the sky with a look of thin fascination and presently he said, "You know, Gene, sometimes I think you're smarter than you let on."

"What's that mean?"

"Who says I won't be on that stage?" Dierkes chuckled and stood up.

It was almost dark by the time the coroner's inquest ended. MacIver left the place at Ethan Scott's shoulder; they crossed the street to the Chinaman's café and ate a meal during which neither man spoke half a dozen words; and afterward they walked to the Nugget. Scott said, "I understand you went to the theater last night."

"Yes."

"I'd like to have gone."

"Why didn't you?"

"I was busy with my grapevine," Scott said distantly. They took a small table by the side wall and ordered drinks; MacIver's practiced glance swept the room with its spreading crowd and he felt the pressure of hot and sweating bodies, of thick whiskey fumes and tobacco smoke. The piano was a sharp cadence hardly audible over the drone of men's voices and the clink of glasses and poker

hips and the occasional sharp cry of a woman's carefully
intentional laughter. Men drifted across the floor past their
table and MacIver found that Scott's glance never stopped
traveling from face to face, seeking in each face the threat
of danger. MacIver said, "You're a lucky man to be alive.
Why not quit this business?"

"No."

"Why?" he insisted.

"Pry into your own soul before you pry into mine,"
Scott said. He was busy scanning the crowd; his eyes
touched MacIver only occasionally. To a casual observer
Scott seemed perfectly at ease, wholly idle. But at all
times at least one of his hands was out of sight beneath the
table; and his eyes never became still. The crowd was
boisterous, laughing strongly, speaking heartily, using up
great quantities of liquor and tobacco. MacIver's gamblers
were busy tonight. Ethan Scott said, "Look at them."

"What?"

"They're all animals."

MacIver smiled briefly. "That's arrogant talk."

"Of course I'm arrogant," Scott murmured. "Otherwise I'd be dead."

"Then where's the difference between you and a man
like Tom Larrabee?"

"Maybe there's none."

"But there is," MacIver disagreed. "There's a difference—I can smell it."

Scott's head lifted momentarily, like an old horse
sensing a mountain lion: he was watching someone across
the room and MacIver thought of impending gunplay, but
when he looked that way, following the direction of Scott's
glance, he saw Marla Searles, dressed in her bright costume, ready to sing. She mounted the dais and stood by
the piano and smiled with vague sweetness down at the
professor. The professor played an arresting chord and
silence came into the room expectantly.

Reluctant to give up his argument, MacIver returned his
attention to Scott and said, "I can still smell the difference."

Scott's answer was a long time coming; he was watching
the dais. Occasionally his glance moved around the room
in precautionary watchfulness. He said, "Don't try to

answer all the world's questions, Krayle. A lot of them are
better left unanswered."

"Hell," MacIver retorted, but he knew by the set of
Scott's head that Scott wasn't listening to him. The professor played an introductory arpeggio and Marla opened her
lips and sang. The songs she sang were Stephen Foster
tunes; Marla's voice was none too good but it was not
Marla's voice that the crowd wanted, so much as it was
just the sight of her. Her face turned slowly and each time
it moved it presented a new beauty, like a new facet of a
diamond turning slowly. MacIver glanced at Scott's profile
and he thought, *Is she the chink in your facade?* The
thought disappointed him. He got to his feet and pushed
through the motionless crowd to the bar, and took a pair of
drinks. He carried them back to the table and sat down; he
saw Scott make a periodic survey of the crowd and return
his intense attention to Marla, and he thought, *You can't
be that much of a fool. She's not for any man.*

Marla's dress was dove-gray, ornamented with sequins
that flashed light around the room in specks. Her auburn
hair fell carelessly around the smooth flesh of her shoulders. Her voice held a song's final note and trailed off; the
professor played his climactic crescendo and Marla dipped
her head, stood still through the violence of miners' ap-
plause, and stepped down off the dais. She moved forward, visible occasionally between milling shapes, holding
her head high and smiling now and then at men who spoke
to her. They opened up to make a path for her and
presently she broke out of the near edge of the crowd and
came toward MacIver's table. Only it was not MacIver
who held her attention; it was Ethan Scott.

MacIver rose and brought up a chair for Marla. She
nodded to him; he said, "You sang well tonight."

"Did I?" Her tone was abstracted. She sat down and
MacIver pushed his own drink toward her, but she shook
her head. She was looking out, at the crowd and past it,
but he knew without question that her mind was on Scott.
She said, without looking toward either of the men, "Five
years is a long time."

And Scott said, "Yes." Scott's head lifted; he looked in
all directions at the crowd, and drew his chair back a few

inches, tilting it back to rest his shoulders against the wall. His attitude was indolent but his right hand hung over the grip of his gun. MacIver felt himself being pushed out of the scene; he held his seat stubbornly. Marla said, "I don't sing well but I like to sing."

"You sing well," Scott murmured. MacIver looked at him but there was no hint of sarcasm in Scott's expression. His eyes displayed no emotion at all; yet they shone quite brightly, intensely.

Marla threw one arm carelessly over the back of her chair and sat that way, slightly turned. MacIver put his eyes on her, not rudely. A lamp was beyond her and the outline of her profile was clear against that light, lovely in detail. The yellow light softened her features and her lips were slightly turned, bittersweet. "A long time," she said in quiet repetition, and moved her face to watch Scott.

There was an almost imperceptible tightness on Scott's cheeks, the surface reflection of his feelings, whatever they were. MacIver saw Scott watching Marla with the same frank appraisal she was giving him. Their glances said things to each other that MacIver didn't catch, and he felt left out, keenly disappointed. There was a slight break in the evenness of Marla's glance; her lips parted slowly, and the dark surfaces of her eyes were touched by a shadow that might have been loneliness.

MacIver thrust himself into it: "I didn't know you two were acquainted."

By way of answer, Marla said, "I hadn't expected to see you again." But she was plainly speaking to Scott, and not MacIver.

"That's strange," Scott said. "I knew we'd meet."

"Did you?"

"We're both camp followers."

"All of us are," MacIver said, almost angrily, but no one paid him any attention. Marla used both palms to smooth her hair back from her temples. She seemed remotely disappointed, perhaps by Scott's answer; yet she said to him, "We're alive, you and I. We always have been. That's what made me. . . ." She stopped. Her eyes touched MacIver but there was no expression in them, not embarrassment or anger or impatience or anything he might have expected her to show; for he thought, with an instant's clear prophetic knowledge, that he could have finished her sentence for her: *That's what made me fall in love with you*. MacIver's puzzled attention shifted from the girl to the man and back again. Scott was looking straight at her; he was saying, "Back along the trail. But you found it was a mistake."

"Yes," she answered. "It was a mistake."

"You proceeded to put your mistake from your thoughts," Scott murmured. "How well did you succeed?"

MacIver knew then that he was an outsider and that none of this was for him; but neither of them objected to his presence and curiosity, that powerful instinct, kept him where he was. He saw an instant blaze of feeling in Marla's eyes in answer to Scott's soft-voiced question; then her face again became solemn and noncommittal. She had always been truthful with MacIver and now, he saw, she was truthful with Scott too. "I don't know," she said.

"Just so," Scott said. He adjusted his weight in the chair and directed a sleepy glance at MacIver. "Krayle says he's a friend of mine."

"I am," MacIver said; he felt color move to his cheeks from being brought so suddenly into the conversation in such an impersonal way.

"If he says so," Marla told Scott, "then it's true."

Scott waved his hand gently. "No matter. I don't wish to bring trouble between us." He said it directly to MacIver; but it was not MacIver who answered, for MacIver didn't understand what he meant. He heard Marla's answer: "You're not hurting him, Ethan."

"Stepping on a man's toes? That hurts most of us."

"You're not stepping on his toes," Marla said, and looked at MacIver. MacIver frowned. Marla said, "Krayle has no claim on me. He never had."

It cleared the issue up for MacIver; at last he understood, and he said, "That's true."

Scott's bleak eyes held MacIver's. "You're sure."

"Yes."

"Very well," Scott said.

MacIver said nothing. He felt the pressure of Scott's glance and Marla's glance and he knew it was their way of asking him to leave, but his stubborn streak was roused and he sat still. *If they want to be alone they can go somewhere else. This is my own saloon, damn it.*

Marla's eyes slid away and he could see they had accepted his refusal to go. They accepted an alternative, which was to ignore his presence again. Once more he was pushed out on the edge of the scene and left hanging there unnoticed. Marla looked at Scott and there was a brightening interest behind her long eyes. Her lips were set in gentle composure and, during the stretching stillness, the powerful wash of something wholly intangible—possibly Scott's thoughts, or Marla's, or both—seemed to cross the space between them, touching MacIver as it passed. The force of it must have struck the girl as well. He saw her eyes become round and her breasts lift with her quickened breathing. Her glance lay steady on Scott, and in response to that nebulous force, the strict lines that had been set around Scott's mouth relaxed just a little. There was no more than that; till Scott, who seldom smiled, showed momentary gentleness. Usually he appeared to MacIver to have the tendency of being hard with himself, but just now his lips were relaxed and his eyes were less brittle when they swept the droning crowd.

Scott touched the points of his mustache and said, "Once there was a good thing."

"Yes," Marla said.

"It began on both sides."

"I was never sure of that," she said.

"Then I'm sorry—it was a failing in me."

"You never let anyone see your feelings," she said.

"Strong habits are hard to break."

"Perhaps you have no feelings to show."

"No," Scott said. "That's wrong. You know it's wrong."

"Do I?"

His gaze held her. "Yes."

Marla's eyes fell to her hands, now folded in her lap; when she looked up again, MacIver turned toward Scott, who was looking away, staring darkly at the mass of miners crowding the bar, absorbed in his own bleak thoughts. Marla said, "What is it?"

"Sometimes," Scott said, so softly that MacIver al-

most missed his words, "I wish I could tell you—I wish I
could tell myself."

"Then talk about it."

"I don't know," he said in a groping way; but his face
remained flat and expressionless. MacIver watched with
breathless interest; he did not stir. "Sometimes," Scott
said, "a man tightens up inside until he can hardly breathe.
What do you do when you want to take a shot at someone
but there's no one around—nothing but air?"

"I'm here," Marla said to him. "Do you want to take a
shot at me?"

Scott's face did not move. MacIver saw him from a
new direction in that moment; he saw within Scott a
frightening, powerful explosive force. He had glimpsed it
before but this was the first time Scott had ever revealed
this much of it.

But now the mask of bitter silence was replaced. Scott
stood up, almost abruptly, and said a brief, "Good night."
And walked away from the table without looking back.

MacIver followed Scott with his eyes until Scott's
figure, almost dapper in the carefully pressed suit, went
out of sight through the door; then MacIver looked at
Marla. "You were in love with him, once."

"Once."

"You still are."

"Perhaps," she said. She was watching the empty
doorway. "Don't get in beyond your depth, Krayle—it can
only bring you grief. I mean that as a friend." She looked
at him very soberly.

"I don't think I follow you," he said.

"That's fine," she said. "Good night, then." She got
up and walked away.

Then MacIver sat nursing his drink, trying to work it
all out in his thoughts. But little of it made sense. Presently he crossed the room and relieved the house gambler at
the faro layout.

VIII

AT TEN-THIRTY that night MacIver left a brisk trade in the Nugget and walked across to stand on the corner by the hardware store. A soft ring of dust lay around the high moon. Squares of lamplight splashed out of windows and fell along the streets sprawling, giving the dusty streets a patchwork appearance.

MacIver removed his hat and let the wind rough up his hair and cool his skin, damp from the close and soporific heat of the crowded saloon. He tarried briefly where he was, his thoughtful eye half on the town and half on his own soul, and then began walking south along the Bow Street walk, his hat making a careless angle across his view. It was a cheerless city, he reflected, made so by the simple presence of one man—Ethan Scott—and that man's challenge to the toughs.

The streets were quiet. Up ahead, a figure came out of a doorway: Tom Larrabee. Energy thrust out of Larrabee even when he stood stock still. Two or three others came out on the walk to join Larrabee. Walking toward them, MacIver heard a swift, low half-minute of talk, during which he recognized the heavy singing of Guy Murvain's voice. Then Murvain and the others headed across the street, leaving Larrabee alone on the walk. Larrabee seemed about to turn away, but then his head swung and he recognized MacIver, and took a solid stance, waiting. MacIver came up to him with a courteous, "'Evening."

Larrabee had an odd, waspish expression. "I understand you took Nita Matlock to the theater last night."

"So I did."

"How were the players?" Larrabee's grim tone belied his idle words.

"Good enough, I suppose." MacIver frowned, uncertain. His last drink hung heavy in his stomach.

"That's fine," Larrabee said smoothly. His attention fell casually on MacIver's face and his tone startled MacIver: "Leave her alone, my friend. She's not for you."

MacIver's answer was quick and sure, and dry: "I don't mean to sound childish, but I guess I'll just leave that up to her. She doesn't have to see me if she doesn't choose to."

"I'll do the choosing," Larrabee said. His talk was harsh and the smell of whiskey was heavy on his breath, heavy enough to have rubbed off some of the man's customary polish.

Plainly holding back a great many things, MacIver looked around while he formed his answer. A dark, crowded mass of saddle ponies waited riderless along the east rim of Bow Street. MacIver let his voice cut forward mildly: "Let's talk about it again when you've got a little less hooch in you, Tom."

It was impossible to anticipate the reactions of Larrabee's seesaw temper. Now he turned halfway around, facing away to the north as if to leave, and said softly, "Maybe you're right."

But he stood that way, looking over his shoulder toward MacIver, arrested in that curious position, and MacIver felt his belly churn, not trusting the man at all. Alert but not sure, he stood fast and awaited Larrabee's next action. Larrabee regarded him with the blank steadiness of alcohol and after a while MacIver smelled the scent of Larrabee's anger clinging to the air along with stale whiskey fumes. Larrabee reversed himself again, coming around to face him, rolling his tall shoulders forward. Larrabee's jaw crept down to clamp into a long level line and his voice was curt: "Mind what I said, MacIver."

MacIver frowned at his thick-tongued arrogance. "Make up your mind, Tom."

And while he watched Larrabee, he thought, *He's all ready to jump*. But he wasn't troubled by it. MacIver was small but he was not soft. He had spent the better part of his life in tough camps and particularly in saloons. He knew all the effective methods of barroom infighting and he knew one other thing: a man as drunk as Larrabee was right now was a man with his reactions slowed down considerably.

Still, he observed himself growing tense. Feeling owded, he disliked the feeling impatiently, and found mself wishing that Larrabee would come to his sluggish cision.

Larrabee lifted his chin. His eyes gleamed distinctly. is shoulders stirred; and he said, "You damned pup!" He ared at MacIver a moment longer, lowered his head and arged.

MacIver sidestepped swiftly, avoiding the intended atting. He let Larrabee plow right on past against the ilding wall. Larrabee bounced back, shaking his head to ear it, and MacIver said to him calmly, "Simmer down, m. You're too drunk to fight."

Larrabee only growled and plowed ahead again, his ms windmilling with wild punches. MacIver dodged back d forth until he saw an opening, which wasn't hard to d. He stepped in and swung a short hook into Larrabee's lly. He had thought it would double the man over, but it d not. Larrabee's stomach muscles were hard and tough d he only grunted a little, wrapping his long, powerful ms around MacIver in a hug that tightened quickly, reatening to cut off MacIver's wind. He felt his ribs giving der that pressure and suddenly, for the first time, hot ger overcame him. His foot lifted and in a swift compound otion he rammed his knee into Larrabee's groin and amped his foot back down against Larrabee's instep.

It broke Larrabee's hold. It sent Larrabee reeling ack, crying out, and in that moment Larrabee was mpletely unguarded—his hands had dropped to cover is injured crotch and he was hopping on one foot. MacIver aped forward with his hands extended, got a firm grip ound the back of Larrabee's head and smashed it down gainst his own lifting knee. He heard something crush— robably the cartilage in Larrabee's nose—and he stepped ack to let Larrabee fall.

Larrabee sprawled on his face and rolled onto his de, doubling his legs, moaning. MacIver stood over him reathing heavily. "Had enough, Tom?"

Larrabee gasped something that sounded affirmative. IacIver watched him a while longer and then started to rn away. When his back was to Larrabee he felt the rise

of the hairs at the base of his neck; his head turned and i
a corner of his vision he caught the glint of metal. H
wheeled, reaching inside his coat, but he knew in
sinking way that he was too late.

Larrabee was more treacherous than he had suspected
Larrabee's gun was already lifting toward him—and then
single gunshot crashed from somewhere behind MacIver

Larrabee did two things: he dropped his gun an
lifted his left hand to clutch his right elbow. His fac
contorted with severe pain.

MacIver wheeled. Out in the middle of the street,
man stood by a riderless horse. Ethan Scott. Scott holstere
his gun and gathered the reins in quick synchronizatio
with his graceful rise to the saddle, and rode forward t
the edge of the walk.

"God," MacIver said, looking back at Larrabee. "
thank you, Ethan."

"I pay my debts," Scott said. "I think the shot smashe
his elbow. He may never use it again."

"God," MacIver said again. "I'm sorry for him, then.

"Why?" Scott lifted his reins.

MacIver shook his head. "You're headed for Spanis
Flat to ride the payroll coach?"

"Yes."

"Maybe I'll join you there. Mind if I travel the stag
with you?"

"I don't mind," Scott said. "Anyone's free to buy
ticket." He wheeled his horse and drummed north alon
the street. Across the way, up in the second-story window o
the hotel, a pair of hands separated the curtains and
woman's figure stood outlined, looking out. That was Marla
The curtains, having parted, closed again, and MacIve
stood watching Scott retreat through the night until hi
horse turned past the church and faded from sight.

MacIver turned back to the walk and knelt by Ton
Larrabee. Larrabee was sitting up, bent over, rocking bac
and forth and moaning while he clutched his shattere
elbow. Tears and blood mixed to stream down his face
MacIver put his hand under the man's shoulder and lifte
him to his feet. "Come on. I'll take you down to Docto
Pohl's."

Larrabee shook him off with weak defiance. "I can get there without your help damn you—you and your killer friend."

Weaving on uncertain legs, Larrabee moved away, going down the street the three doors to the doctor's office. He banged on the door and didn't wait for an answer, but rammed right inside and shut the door loudly behind him. MacIver knelt to retrieve his hat from where it had fallen on the walk. He dusted it off, put it on his head, and held the doctor's door with his gaze for a moment. He had made another mistake tonight—underestimating Larrabee. *Making too many mistakes lately. I'm not liable to live through too many more of them. Better tighten up, MacIver.*

Still, it taught him one more thing about Tom Larrabee. Larrabee refused to lose a fight. It was one of many lessons MacIver was learning these days.

He turned back upstreet, looking at his watch and finding it was ten forty-five. The sheriff would be making his evening rounds now, and would probably be found in Turk Chaffee's small, subdued but proper saloon. MacIver crossed Third and continued up the Bow Street walk to Chaffee's and went in there.

Chaffee was tending bar himself. When he saw MacIver his thin face lighted up in a derisive smile. "Get rolled by one of your own drunks, Mac?"

MacIver didn't bother to make an answer. All he said was, "Sheriff Castillo been here?"

"Been here," Chaffee said, "still here. In back somewhere."

"Obliged," MacIver drawled, and threaded tables to get back through the long, narrow room. Several poker games were going, all of them patronized by the town's upper class of customers, and he found the sheriff kibitzing one game. He touched the sheriff's thick arm and said, "I'd like to talk to you."

"All right," the sheriff said incuriously, and walked around the table to the back end of the room, where he opened a door and let himself out into the alley. MacIver followed and shut the door. The sheriff said, "This private enough?"

"It'll do. I wanted to tell you before Larrabee does. Larrabee got drunk tonight and decided he'd try me on with his fists."

"And?"

"He tried."

The sheriff's fat face showed very mild surprise. "You licked him, then."

"Yes. But he's a little brash. When I turned my back he pulled a gun on me."

The sheriff's hatbrim lifted sharply. MacIver caught the faint glint of light on his eyes. "You killed him?"

"I'm no gunman," MacIver said. "I never shot anybody in my life."

"Then what is it you're trying to tell me?"

"Ethan Scott saw Larrabee drawing his gun. Scott put a bullet through Larrabee's elbow. It took the fight out of him—he's down at Doctor Pohl's."

"I see," the sheriff said. "And where's Scott?"

"Rode to Spanish Flat. I guess he wants a few hours' sleep before he boards the stage in the morning."

The sheriff nodded. "I'm planning to meet him there."

"Look," MacIver told him, "Larrabee may get ugly and decide to swear out a complaint against me, Sheriff. But I won't have it."

"You won't have what?"

"No warrant," MacIver said evenly. "Understand me?"

"*Un momento*," the sheriff murmured. He was obviously flustered; he only lapsed into Spanish when he was taken by surprise. "Are you trying to dictate my job to me, señor?"

"No warrant," MacIver said bluntly, and turned on his heel, walking away. He went south to the end of the alley, turned east and walked to Bow Street, and crossed the intersection to the Nugget. A quartet of cowboys from some ranch out in the valley breasted the end of Third Street and swept forward toward him, their cantering horses drumming the earth, their hats lifted and their cheerful shouts undulating forward through the town. MacIver entered the saloon with his face turned into a glowering frown. When he looked back he saw that this was not the first time Tom Larrabee had given him trouble; and he knew it meant more than just a fight between two individuals. Larrabee was one side of the town and MacIver was the other. The battle for control had opened.

He took a quick drink at the bar, dusted off his coat as best he could, and went back to the door. He stood aside to let the four boisterous cowboys come in; then he went out, crossed the street once more and went south along Bow. When he walked past the doctor's office he looked inside but the windows were curtained off. He continued downstreet another block and, at a few minutes after eleven, curled his bantam form into Nita Matlock's café.

Nita was alone in the room. "I was about to close."

"I know," he said. "I'll walk you home, if you don't mind."

"All right." He couldn't tell the meaning behind her slight smile. The girl untied her apron and hung it away, and walked to the door. MacIver waited for her to lock it; then she put her hand through his arm and they walked up to the corner and then slowly west along the tree-shadowed walks of Fourth. MacIver said, "I just had a fight with Tom Larrabee." A small pride lifted in him.

"I suppose it would be foolish of me to ask what it was about," Nita said.

"You've got a little of the coquette in you, haven't you?"

"All women do," she said, smiling in the dark. MacIver turned his head toward her. She said, "I hope Tom wasn't hurt."

"Ethan Scott put a bullet in his arm. It may have wrecked his elbow."

"Oh," she said quickly, with a little gasp of breath. "I'm sorry—that's cruel. Why did Scott shoot him?"

MacIver hesitated; but there would be no use in not telling the truth. "He was about to backshoot me."

She didn't reply for a moment. Then her face moved. "Yes. Tom would be capable of that."

"Ah," he said. "Bright girl."

"Is Ethan Scott a friend of yours?"

"That's a deep question," he answered, and considered it. "I think he is—he claims he's not."

"Why?"

"He says," MacIver began, and paused; "he says he has no friends."

"Then I'm sorry for him, too."

"Aye," he murmured. They reached the end of the block, crossed a dusty cross street and went on into the next block. He spoke again suddenly: "Maybe I've made a mistake. I don't mean to trespass on Tom Larrabee's property."

"Oh?" she said, softly laughing at him. "If I were his property, would I have turned him down and then gone with you to the theater last night?"

He glanced at her curiously. "I don't know what you'd do."

"That's frank enough," she said, and laughed again. "I'm simpler than you think I am. I'm not Tom's property—I never was."

"He says you are."

"Tom says a lot of things. Much of the time he's wrong."

They walked on slowly in a thickness of silence until they came to the gate of her little house; she stopped there and looked at him quite soberly. "Perhaps I should ask you the same question."

"What question?"

"Am I trespassing?"

"I see," he said. "You're thinking of Marla Searles."

"Yes."

"Marla is a businesswoman. She's associated with me in certain business dealings and she sings at the Nugget. That's all."

"You're sure?"

"Quite sure," he said. He couldn't keep all the dryness out of his tone. "If she has a man it isn't me."

She considered him at some length. She held her strong, soft-rounded shape quite still and through the faint light she had a growing power—he couldn't tell if it was a conscious one—a power to attract him. She said, "Come inside. I'll fix some coffee."

"I can use it." He followed her up the walk, across the porch and into the little parlor. She told him to sit down; she went across the room to the stove, opened the door, kindled a fire, and set a small coffeepot on the lid of the stove. "I have no kitchen."

"I shouldn't think you would," he observed, and thought of her café.

She laughed softly and when the fire lifted she closed the stove door and came back across the width of the room to take a seat on a chair nearby, regarding him a little quizzically. "You're sure about what you said a minute ago, about Marla Searles?"

"Why press the point?" he countered.

"Because I suspect she has a hold on you," the girl said.

"Well," he answered, "maybe she did, once."

"Then that's what I see—the ashes of it."

"Yes," he said. "No more than that."

She nodded, as though deep in thought; she sat with her arms idle for a moment longer and then went to the stove, lifting the coffeepot's lid and letting the coffee's smell rise to her nostrils. "All ready," she said to herself, and took the coffeepot off the stove. Somewhere across town a man's voice rose in a sustained roar of laughter, clearly audible even at this distance. MacIver's head turned slightly toward the open window. Nita said, "That's another world, over there."

"Why," he said, "I suppose it is." His head turned back and he accepted a cup of coffee from her and watched her sit down. "But I see the town from that side. You see some of it too, during the day."

"I suppose I do," she said. Her face held a quiet, sweet-lipped gravity. "But when you work on the dividing line, as I do, you learn something—men are all the same."

He shook his head. "Not in this town."

"Why do you believe that?"

"Because I live on the other side," he answered. He didn't choose to pursue this point with her, and so he shifted the subject, saying, "I don't like to see you working on Bow Street."

"My place is on this side of the street."

"Just the same, it's too close to the line."

"What of it?" she said.

"Do you like them watching you all the time?"

"I don't mind," she said. "What can they see?"

"What image does a thirsty man see?"

She shook her head. "You're taking too much on yourself."

He subsided. "My apologies."

"No. I think you ought to understand. I have to make my own way—I run a restaurant. If a man wants more than that, then Madam Yvette's is across the street. You see?"

"I'm sorry," he said again. "It wasn't my place to pry."

"Why," she murmured, watching him with interest, "I'd be disappointed if you weren't concerned."

"Would you?"

"Yes."

"Then," he said, "it's all right, isn't it?"

She smiled. "We're both lonely people, aren't we? We're both mavericks—and it's all right."

He felt a measure of relief; he lifted his coffee cup in gentle toast, and watched her gravely over the rim of the cup while he drank.

IX

WITH THE SUN only half an hour high, MacIver stood on the cindered railroad platform of Spanish Flat beside Ethan Scott, watching four men carry the payroll chest from the express car across the depot platform to the waiting Butterfield coach. Standing beside the coach was the fat figure of Sheriff Eugenio Castillo. The driver stood talking with the sheriff, and MacIver noticed Ethan Scott's glance flick in that direction. MacIver said, "I wonder what possessed the sheriff to risk his neck today?"

"I have an idea," Scott said, "but I'll keep it to myself. Just keep him downwind of me."

"What?"

"If we're held up, keep your eye on him. I don't want him to have a chance at my back."

"You don't trust him at all, do you?"

"I trust no one," Scott murmured. He settled his shoulders and swung toward the stage, and spoke to the driver: "Any other passengers today?"

"Just the sheriff here and Mr. MacIver. They all heard about the payroll, Mr. Scott—nobody wanted to take the chance."

Scott regarded the stubble-faced driver bleakly. "You're scared too?"

"No, sir. Not me. Not with you ridin' shotgun."

"That's fine," Scott said in an arid tone. "Get inside, Sheriff."

The sheriff climbed inside the coach, offering no argument. MacIver followed him and got settled, and felt the coach body lurch when the driver and Scott put their weight on the side of it, climbing up to the high seat. Then the crush of boots reported forward from the platform cinders, running boots, and MacIver leaned forward to look out. Rushing across the depot was a tall, redheaded man: Henry Dierkes.

"Well," MacIver breathed, and looked directly at the sheriff. "I'll be double-damned!"

"Think of that," the sheriff said, looking out the window.

"Wait a minute!" Dierkes called, and ran up beside the stagecoach. "I got me a ticket too."

There was a brief silence. Then MacIver heard Ethan Scott's calm tones: "Then get inside, Henry."

The door swung open and Dierkes heaved his tall body into the coach. He looked around, saw the sheriff, and then stopped when his glance fell on MacIver. His eyes narrowed and his hands became still. "Well," he said. "Well."

"'Morning," MacIver drawled. Dierkes took a seat beside the sheriff, across from MacIver. Dierkes grinned. The sheriff said, "You sure as hell have got gall, Henry."

"It's a free country," Dierkes said, in the manner of a parrot.

"Maybe," MacIver said skeptically.

Dierkes grinned at him. "I'm entitled to passage on this stagecoach same as anybody else, MacIver."

"As you say," MacIver muttered. His hand rested

under the lapel of his coat, gently clasped around the butt of his short gun. The sheriff, he noticed, carried a shotgun— good for close work, but useless at any distance. It was enough to make MacIver pause for thought.

Henry Dierkes carried his two revolvers at his thighs. His arms were folded across his chest. Up above, the driver whooped and cracked his whip and the coach jerked forward, rocking and tossing the passengers around on the seats.

"You know," MacIver observed, "the sheriff's right, Henry. A man can't help but admire your guts."

Henry's grin was easy. "Then we're even, my friend. I kind of admire the way you stopped Raven cold the other day. I'd even admire to see you try it again."

"If I have to," MacIver murmured. "Tell me something, Henry. You intend to hold up this stage?"

"Me?" Dierkes threw his head back, laughing. "Why, I never hold up stagecoaches—it ain't good for the health. And I prize my health."

"I've noticed that. I took particular notice of it the other afternoon when you walked out of the Nugget before the ruckus started."

For a brief instant Dierkes's eyes turned ugly and mean; but then he laughed again, softly. "I had nothin' to do with that little party, MacIver. I just came in to pay my respects to my old friend Scott. I did it and I left. What's yellow about that?"

"Nothing, when you tell it that way." MacIver lapsed into silence; so did Dierkes. MacIver caught the sheriff's nervous glance searching the countryside that lurched by on the sides of the road. *He's jumpy enough,* MacIver thought. *Would he be that jumpy if he was really tied in with Henry? I wonder if Ethan isn't wrong about him. Funny, the way suspicion shifts around.*

"I noticed," he said aloud, "it took four men to haul that payroll box onto the stage. How come it's that heavy?"

"On purpose," the sheriff said. He looked at Dierkes. "No man on horseback could get away with a box that heavy."

Dierkes regarded the sheriff with an insolent stare. "Somebody might blow the box open and take what's in it. You thought of that, Sheriff?"

The sheriff stiffened and looked uncomfortably at

MacIver. *Either he's honest,* MacIver thought, *or he's doing a damn good job of playing a role.*

The coach bucked and squeaked on its leather springs. By eight o'clock they were well down the road, heading straight south below the Mogul Rim on the last hour's stretch to Lodestar. If there was to be a holdup, it would be around here somewhere; and so thinking, MacIver increased his vigilance. He did not watch the country passing by—he left that up to Ethan Scott on the high seat. MacIver kept his attention on Henry Dierkes, with a little corner of it devoted to the sheriff.

The sheriff spoke up: "Tom Larrabee wanted me to swear out a warrant against you."

Dierkes put a curious glance toward the sheriff but the sheriff ignored him. MacIver said, "Thanks for not serving it."

The sheriff chuckled. "Give me credit for one thing, Mac—I know which side the butter's on."

MacIver considered him. "Which would lead me to think you don't figure Larrabee will last as long as I do."

The sheriff smiled. "What do *you* think?"

MacIver shrugged in answer. It was Henry Dierkes who offered argument: "I wouldn't count on it, MacIver." And that one simple statement gave MacIver pause for a good deal of thought.

That was when the toughs made their try.

They came in a bunch, seven or eight of them, rushing forward along the road in front of the stage in a tight-packed group, forcing the stage to stop or collide. It stopped. The toughs wore bandanna masks tied across their noses in the manner of trail-herd drag riders. One of them carried his arm in a sling—would that be Arnie? MacIver had time to see that much before he palmed his gun and brought it out into sight and let its muzzle lie pointed at the two men in the seat opposite. "Don't anybody move."

The sheriff glared at him in sudden hot anger. "What the Hell—are you one of them?"

"I don't want our shotgun guard killed from behind," MacIver murmured.

"Hell," the sheriff retorted, "I can't even see Scott. But I sure as hell can see some of those rawhiders."

"All right," MacIver decided. "But not you, Henry."

"I'm just mindin' my own business," Dierkes murmured smugly.

There had been, up to now, a lull in the activity outside the coach. Apparently the toughs and Scott had been sizing each other up. Now, just as the sheriff turned heavily toward the open window with his shotgun, an abrupt burst of fire crashed across the silence. Gunfire warmed up the air and a good amount of it seemed to issue from the seat above MacIver's head: Scott must be handling his share of it. But MacIver didn't turn to look. A bullet ricochetted from the wood not far from his head and he flinched away from it, but kept his gun and his eyes on Henry Dierkes, just as he had on Raven the other night in the Nugget. Dierkes smiled insolently and sat wholly still. The sheriff had lifted his shotgun and now poked it out the window, firing one shot and then a second and peering through the smoke trying to find his targets. "Missed, damn it!"

The harsh talk of gunfire rose and fell; men's high shouts sailed past—and then suddenly the toughs rushed away in a body, thundering from the road, and stillness settled over the coach.

MacIver said, "I'll take your guns, Henry. Just to make sure."

"All right," Dierkes said indolently. He unbuckled his belt and dropped it on the floor of the coach, nudging it toward MacIver with his boot toe.

Then MacIver gestured with his gun. "Outside."

The sheriff and Dierkes stepped out. MacIver followed and immediately looked up at the box. "You all right?"

"I am," Scott said. "The driver's not. Give me a hand."

MacIver climbed up on the front wheel hub. The driver sat slumped over, clutching his leg; blood welled slowly from a wound in his thigh. MacIver helped Scott lower him to the ground. The driver stood weakly against the side of the coach shaking his head. Scott glanced at the man's wound and said to Henry Dierkes, "Your boys are bad shots, bucko."

"I didn't recognize any of 'em," Dierkes said with bland cheeks.

The driver was muttering. "Judas, I never seen anything like that. Hell, Mr. Scott—you put up as much of a fight as all of them put together. I never saw one man fire so much ammunition in such a short time. Judas."

Scott wasn't listening. He was walking out to the rim of the road where a man was down, one of the toughs. Scott's coattails flapped gently as he walked. He crouched and rolled the man over and MacIver saw the sling on the dead man's arm. When Scott jerked the man's mask down it revealed the face of the squat tough, Arnie. Scott walked back to the coach and put his hollow glance on Henry Dierkes. "Recognize him now?"

"I guess I do."

"How many's it going to have to be, Henry?"

Dierkes shrugged. "Everybody has his time. Chicken today, feathers tomorrow. Arnie wasn't much good."

"Neither are you."

Dierkes flushed. "I'll take exception to that, Ethan, if you don't mind."

"I don't mind."

MacIver caught no sign of feeling on Scott's face. Scott said, "This is pretty raw, Henry. With your hired hand dead on the ground over there, do you still claim you had nothing to do with this?"

Dierkes's face didn't lose its desperately forced grin. "You didn't see me shoot, did you? Hell, ask Arnie if I had anything to do with it." His grin widened. "Go ahead. Ask him."

MacIver said, "I'm a little tired of your brand of humor, Henry."

"Well, now, Mr. MacIver, I reckon that's just too bad. I'm sorry to hear you talk that way."

"Aagh," MacIver murmured in disgust and turned away. He heard Dierkes, still talking behind him:

"You gents can go on without me. I guess I ought to stay and bury Arnie."

"And then walk home?" MacIver said, swinging around. "It's twenty miles from here to your place."

"I'll make it," Dierkes said. "I like to walk."

"Hell," the stage driver said, "I'll bet he's got a horse cached around here."

Dierkes shook his head. "Afraid not, Pete. If I staked out a horse in this neck of the woods, it'd be as good as admitting I knew where you'd get held up. But don't you folks worry about me. I'd just as soon not ride into town with you anyway. I ain't too popular in Lodestar these days."

So saying, Dierkes walked away. He stooped by Arnie's body and picked it up and walked over the hill out of sight, carrying the dead man.

When he was gone Ethan Scott turned to confront the sheriff. "I noticed you did a lot of shooting but you didn't manage to hit much."

The sheriff colored. "When did you get time to notice anything?"

"Sheriff," Scott said quietly, "let me make myself understood. If you ever put yourself in my road I'll ride you down. On your shirt that badge isn't worth a penny. I've been hired to clean up this district and I'll do it with or without your help—but if you try to hinder me I'll probably have to kill you."

Scott turned abruptly and nodded to Pete, the driver, and helped him inside the stage. Then he turned to MacIver. "Know how to drive a team?"

"I can try," MacIver said, and climbed up on the box. Scott picked up his rifle, jacked a shell into the chamber and said to the sheriff, "Get in."

The sheriff hauled his heavy weight inside. Scott came up to settle beside MacIver on the high seat. MacIver threaded the reins through his fingers, let the brake off and clucked to the horses. The team lunged forward, broke the stage cleanly from a standstill to a trot, and went down the road without the need of guidance. While they clattered forward, MacIver spoke slowly: "How many more of those do you expect to live through?"

"I never expect to live through them," Scott answered. His tone was quite conversational.

"Then why set yourself up as a target?"

Scott didn't make an immediate answer. Finally he said, "I've got to." And that was all.

MacIver shook his head gently. There was no understanding Scott. Presently his mind struck another subject and he said, "I'm not as sure as you are about the sheriff. He said some things in the coach that made me think he might be more dumb than dishonest."

"That's one of your faults," Scott said, "putting too much trust in too many people. I caught a look that passed between Dierkes and the sheriff back there. To my mind it put them together like brothers."

"I don't agree," MacIver said. "Tom Larrabee wanted the sheriff to swear out a warrant against me for beating him up last night, and one against you for the shooting. The sheriff refused to serve them."

"What does that prove?"

"It seems to mean the sheriff isn't working for Larrabee, if Larrabee's the man behind all this outlawry."

"It doesn't prove that at all. If you were Larrabee, and if you were heading up that bunch, would you let a man like the sheriff in on it? I'd guess you probably wouldn't. The sheriff gets his orders from Henry Dierkes and that's as much as he knows. He may not ever have suspected that anybody's behind Dierkes."

"Maybe," MacIver said skeptically. "Listen, Henry said he thought Larrabee would outlive me. He said it in a way that led me to think he and Larrabee are more friendly than they'd like to have us think."

"That proves nothing either," Scott said. "In case you don't realize it, Dierkes wants you dead. He hasn't forgotten that you sided with me against his crew in that fracas the other night. After today he'll probably send men after you. It's no surprise he'd bet on Larrabee's outliving you."

"That's a point," MacIver conceded.

"It might be wise for you to sell out and leave."

"No. I told you before, I'm staying to see the fun."

"Is there ever any fun?"

"I don't know," MacIver said. "But I've got a stake in this now."

"What stake?"

MacIver shrugged; and when Scott looked at him, Scott said, "A woman?"

"Maybe," MacIver said. He felt Scott's eyes on him and when he turned that way, he thought he saw troubled signs in Scott's gray eyes.

* * *

Coming up Third to the intersection of Bow Street, MacIver paused and regarded both sides of the line with a bit of nervousness. He saw a huge shape standing under the arch of the livery stable, partly concealed in shadow— Sheriff Eugenio Castillo, keeping his indolent eye on the town. Down the other way, where the Lodgepole offices fronted on the walk, Tom Larrabee stood, his tall body motionless, his arm in a heavy white sling and cast. Larrabee was so far away that it was impossible to tell whether his eyes were on MacIver or not, but Larrabee's head gave a queer little jerk and he turned with an abrupt snap of his body and came up the street. MacIver didn't wait for him. There was no business to attend to. He went across the street into the Nugget and found Ethan Scott sitting over a solitaire game half completed. "Well," MacIver said, "it's started. I told you it would start."

Scott looked up from his solitaire board. "What's started?"

"The vultures," MacIver said. "I carry a message from Guy Murvain. He's holding a meeting of the mine owners' combine at his house. He wants you. I included myself in the invitation. Murvain didn't seem to mind."

"Now?"

"Yes."

"All right," Scott said, showing no surprise and no irritation. He swept the cards together into a pack and took his hat and stood up from the table. On the way past the bar he left the pack of cards. MacIver went outside with him and west along Third the three blocks to Murvain's house.

Murvain's was the biggest private house in Lodestar. It was a two-story affair, part stone, part lumber and part 'dobe, with a galleried porch running the length of the front, supported by Georgian pillars. Sycamores and elms shaded the house and grounds. Out back was a stable and another building that enclosed servants' quarters. Murvain's property occupied most of this block of ground, making it plain that the resident was a man of importance.

They walked up the gravel drive and MacIver yanked the bellpull by the door.

A woman admitted them, a stiff-backed woman with

her hair done straight back from her forehead. MacIver said, "Mrs. Murvain—Ethan Scott."

Scott removed his hat and dipped his head. The woman nodded curtly and turned her back, going directly to the staircase and up. MacIver chuckled. "That's just a sample. They don't like us over here on this side of the line."

"They never do."

"Don't you care?"

"No."

"This way, then," MacIver said, and led the way to the side of the big entrance hallway, through a door into Murvain's massive study. Perhaps half a dozen men were here, most of the members of the combine, and that included Murvain—and Tom Larrabee. Larrabee looked across the room at them from his seat and clamped his lips tightly together. MacIver met his belligerent stare with a mild glance, almost derisive.

Murvain had seated his powerful body in a thronelike chair by the massive stone fireplace. Now he lifted his cigar and indicated chairs for MacIver and Scott. "Sit down, gentlemen. I think we can begin the meeting now."

"By all means, do," MacIver murmured caustically. It was not for MacIver's ears. Murvain stood up and paced pretentiously back and forth, his cigar jutting from his rosebud mouth and his hands clasped behind his rump. "Gentlemen, I think it's plain that a vote of thanks is due Mr. Scott for foiling the attempted robbery of the stagecoach two days ago. This action has put the first crack in Henry Dierkes's armor in months. Now that the Mountain King payroll has safely passed the lines of the toughs, the men who work for all of us have been heartened and encouraged. They're not ready to quit us cold, as they were a week ago, and we must concede this small part of the victory to Mr. Scott—and, of course, his friend Mr. MacIver."

Murvain added the last as an obvious afterthought. MacIver aimed a small grin at Scott. Scott's cheeks remained enigmatic as iron.

"However," Murvain said, and paused importantly. *Here it comes*, MacIver thought. *I can anticipate him word for word.*

Murvain said, "However, I think certain facts should

be pointed out to you, Mr. Scott, and—yes, to you also, MacIver."

Scott's head lifted an inch. He displayed no interest whatever in the proceedings. "Go on, Mr. Murvain."

"Yes," MacIver murmured under his breath. "Don't keep us all in suspense." He caught Scott's quick side-glance and he subsided.

Murvain continued. "I think you ought to realize, Mr. Scott, that when I hire a man, I expect him to be loyal to his hire. The same is true of every man in this room. Now, you were hired by the combine of mine owners of Lodestar, and Mr. Larrabee happens to be a member of the combine. A rather powerful member, as it happens. Is it loyalty, Mr. Scott, to take a shot at your employer?"

Scott's eyes flicked to the cast on Larrabee's arm, and back to Murvain. "He's lucky to be alive," Scott said expressionlessly.

Murvain flushed. "Is it loyalty, sir?"

"That's a ludicrous question," Scott said mildly. "I don't see any reason why I should answer it. If you have any charges to level against me, level them—and then I'll answer them if I can."

Murvain blinked and lifted his arms, and let them drop. "What's wrong with the question?"

"Every man in this room knows what happened to Larrabee and why it happened. Or if you don't know, you should take the trouble to find out before you come complaining to me."

Tom Larrabee looked weak but game. "Now wait just a minute—"

"I was speaking to Mr. Murvain," Scott said softly. His eyes had not left Murvain's face.

Murvain said, "I think we know what happened that night. But just to make the record clear, you might tell us your version, Mr. Scott."

"Larrabee was drunk. He started a fight with MacIver and MacIver knocked him down. Larrabee pulled a gun on MacIver's back and I shot him."

Murvain considered him steadily. "That's not exactly the way Larrabee tells it."

"What does Larrabee say?" Scott's tone implied that he had no real interest in what Larrabee said and no real interest in what any of them might think of him.

"He says MacIver drew a gun on him first."

"Then Mr. Larrabee is a liar." Scott's tone was very soft and very mild.

Larrabee stiffened in his chair. "Hold it, Scott!"

Scott only glanced at him. He didn't speak; and after a moment Larrabee sank back in the chair, avoiding Scott's eyes.

Murvain still stood centered in the floor, indecision on his face. Finally he pushed his bluff. "Be all that as it may," he said, "the fact remains that you shot Larrabee, and Larrabee is one of the men who employ you. How do you plan to guarantee you won't do the same to any of us?"

"I won't guarantee it," Scott answered. "If one of you throws down on me or a friend of mine I'll do the same thing again."

It was the phrase *friend of mine* that brought MacIver's head around in surprise. But Murvain was speaking again: "That's not much of a bond, Scott."

"Perhaps. It's the way I live, peculiar as it may seem." MacIver sensed a slight contempt in Scott's otherwise courteous tone. "Do you want to fire me?"

Murvain's face darkened. "No one's said anything about firing you. Don't get thin-skinned."

Scott only said again, "Do you want to fire me?"

"No, damn it. But I don't see much loyalty in a man who demands to be let free to shoot up the town and threatens to quit every time he's called to task for it."

"I see," Scott murmured. He stood up, then, and every eye in the room focused a cone of attention on him. His gray glance was bleak and his hands lay still by his sides, and he spoke quite softly:

"No man can hire my loyalty. My loyalty is to myself alone. What you've paid for is not loyalty but the performance of a job—and I'm performing that job. Mr. Murvain, when I took the job it was with the understanding that I would clean up this district—my way. My way includes shooting any man who steps out of line, including members of this combine or anyone else, be it Henry Dierkes or Sheriff Castillo or your local padre. That's my way, Mr. Murvain—and if it doesn't suit you, then best you send me on my way and find yourselves an errand boy who's willing to kowtow to the whims of drunks and fools. It's that simple, sir—and I'll say once more, take me on that basis or not at all."

He had never lifted his voice beyond its normal pitch. It was not a threat, it was a statement; but a thinly disguised disgust lay behind it, and every man in the room knew it. It shamed some of them. Murvain was too full of bluster and bravado to admit he had been outtalked, but he backed down. "All right," he said. "You'll have it your way, Mr. Scott, just as long as you produce the kind of results you've been hired to produce. But if you don't, then you had better take your own advice and quit the country."

"That's understood," Scott said. "But until that time comes, anyone who stands in my way is there at his own risk."

Just that curtly, he swung on his heel and departed.

Surprised, MacIver hurried to catch up with him. On the sidewalk he came alongside Scott and said, "That was pretty, Ethan. I'm glad I was there to see it."

Scott looked at him dismally. "Are you?"

It shut MacIver up long enough for them to traverse a full block. Then he said, "They'll justify a wholesale slaughter with the right ends, won't they?"

"The vultures," Scott said. "The vultures can justify anything with anything."

"What makes them that way, I wonder?"

"They've got an anthill instinct," Scott said. "Left alone they'd be all right. But when they organize they do it in the name of pious principles that are all wrong. Our history is full of men acting in behalf of other men according to pious principles—and every one of their acts brought grief to themselves and someone else. We're not ants—and that's what they don't see. We're individuals, all of us. The only thing that makes us different from animals is that we're individuals—and their pious principles try to destroy that. The more they organize themselves, the more they ruin their own chances—yet they never see it."

"Well," MacIver said, and trailed off, trying to make sense of what Scott had said. They entered the Nugget and Scott went across the room with a deck of cards to resume his solitaire game as though nothing had interrupted him. MacIver took a beer and then, disturbed, went over to the table and sat without waiting for an invitation. "You know, I've been thinking about that stage holdup. Doesn't it seem strange to you that the toughs gave up so easily?"

"Not strange at all," Scott said. "They were only a cover for Dierkes. He and the sheriff were supposed to get me and the driver from behind while I was fighting off the main party. They didn't anticipate you coming along."

MacIver frowned. "That's kind of hard on the sheriff, isn't it?"

Scott's head turned. "Even now, you still trust that hairpin, don't you?"

"Let's just say I haven't got evidence to make me distrust him."

"You'll get in trouble that way," Scott muttered.

"Maybe. Look, did you mean what you said back in the meeting about your friends?"

"What?"

"You said you'd protect your friends, and you seemed to mean me."

"Figure of speech," Scott said.

"No. I don't think I quite believe that. I'm inclined to suspect you're not quite as hard as you pretend to be."

Scott swept him with a cold and deadly stare. "It would be a bad mistake for you ever to think that," he said softly.

X

SCOTT'S BLACK HEAD was motionless. He touched the points of his cavalry-style mustache and said, "On the stagecoach, Krayle said he was staying in Lodestar because he has a stake in it. A woman."

"Did he say that?" Marla's tone showed only polite interest.

"Don't play childish games."

She chuckled. "You're showing your humanity, Ethan."

"Am I?"

She said, "Maybe Krayle has a girl."

"What girl? You?"

"Ethan," she said softly, "your guts are showing, old friend."

Scott turned his rock-hard stare to the window and parted the curtains to look out into the night. While his back was to her the girl said, "You're the first man I've ever allowed in this room with me."

"Honored," he murmured. He turned around and she saw no hint of sarcasm in his expression. Marla sat down on the bed, leaning back against the headboard with her legs stretched out on the quilt and her feet crossed and her hands clasped in her lap. Her lips were set bitter-sweet. Scott said, "What girl, Marla?"

"He's been seeing a lot of Nita Matlock lately."

"She runs a café, doesn't she?"

"Yes."

He turned. "You're sure."

"I'm sure of nothing," she said. "One thing I'm almost certain of is that I've never given Krayle the slightest reason to think he had a claim on me."

"With Krayle," Scott observed, "it doesn't take much more than a slight reason. In some ways he's quite foolish."

"Yes," she said, smiling softly. "But you like him, don't you?"

"Perhaps," he admitted. "But I'd never say it to his face."

She shook her head. "Sometimes I think you're the strangest man on earth, Ethan."

"Perhaps I am."

"At least, your shell's the thickest."

"Is it?"

"Don't you care what anyone thinks of you?"

"No."

"You ought to care."

"I can't help that," he droned.

"Would you, if you could?"

"Sometimes I'd like to."

"Like right now," she said.

"Yes."

"Then why don't you?"

He put his gray stare on her. In any other man it would have been no more than a blank look; in him it represented a look of agony. He said, "I'd appreciate it if we changed the subject."

"No," she said. "For a great many years I've wanted a look under that shell of yours, and this is the first chance I've ever had to peel back a corner of it. I won't quit now."

"Then I'd better leave."

"No. You won't leave."

"No?"

She watched him speculatively for an instant and then said definitely. "No. You want to know if I can do it. You've got to know. You've got to be sure of yourself. You know that if you ever lose your confidence, your arrogant armor that keeps you so supremely sure of yourself, then you're dead. And you've got to stay here now because you've got to prove to yourself that I can't make you lose it."

"God," he said dismally, sitting down slowly on the divan. "I think I'm already dead, Marla."

"You've been fighting it a long time, haven't you?"

"I guess I have." He leaned forward with his elbows on his knees and lowered his face into his hands. "Go ahead," he said. "Pry away."

She stood up and moved across the room, and turned the lamp down. Then she, too, looked out past the curtains at the starlit night; and then she stood by the window, watching him. Presently his head lifted. Something in her eyes must have prompted him to say, "Are you feeling sorry for me?"

"No. Perhaps I should, but I don't. It isn't pity."

"Then why hesitate?"

Her face moved. "I'm not sure." Her long hair tossed slowly back and forth and came to rest.

Scott sat back and lay one arm along the arm of the

divan. Marla turned, folding her arms. "Do you know what makes a man a gunfighter, Ethan?"

"I know what made me one. I can't speak for the others."

"What was it?"

"I was a wild kid. I had to prove how tough I was."

She nodded slowly. "You proved it."

"I'd have been left better off if I hadn't. I wish someone had whipped me. Someone should have killed me."

She said, "That's putting it a little hard."

He made no answer; she said, "Are you afraid of death?"

"No."

"That's what makes a gunfighter," she said. "A man can kill only if he's unafraid of death. It gives him the edge."

"I've seen a lot of killers die afraid."

"Killers, perhaps. But not gunfighters. There's a difference, isn't there?"

"Of course," Scott muttered. "You know a lot about us, don't you?"

"I loved a gunfighter," she answered. "Ethan, why aren't you afraid to die?"

"What's there to fear? There are times when I'd welcome it."

"Do you know what death is?"

"Yes."

"Most of us don't."

"That's what makes them afraid," he said. "I know what it is."

"What, then?"

"Nothing," he replied.

She kept her eyes on him, not quite understanding, and he said, "That's all—it's nothing. I'm not afraid of darkness—why fear dying?"

"That's so comforting," she murmured. "I wish I could believe it. There's a difference between hoping it's true, and believing it."

"I don't believe it," he said. "I know it." ·

"I see that."

"Come here," he said to her.

Her face lifted and without speaking she came forward, settled beside him on the divan and turned her head toward him. "You loved a gunfighter," he murmured. "You still do."

"No."

"You still do," he repeated. His eyes were blank and his tone was quiet.

Her face turned away. "How could I love a stone wall? It's not true," she said. Her fists closed in her lap. "It's not."

"Yes."

Her eyes dropped and she looked at her hands, and opened them. When she looked at him again she only said a single word, a little hopelessly, in a faraway voice. "Ethan."

Twenty minutes before noon, with an angry glower and a firm and measured step, MacIver turned west on Second and went the half-block to the weathered office of the *Lodestar Daily Compass*. MacIver carried a folded newspaper under his arm. He twisted the door latch and and walked right on in without bothering to knock, and stood before the scarred counter across which editor Price Lafayette did business.

Farther back in the room was the big handpress, the stacks of newsprint and racks of handset type and files of back issues of the *Compass* turning yellow, and the tall, baldheaded figure of Price Lafayette. Lafayette was giving instructions to his aproned printer. Now he turned and seeing MacIver nodded and called, "Be with you shortly, MacIver," and turned back to his conversation with the printer.

MacIver's lips drew tighter with impatience; the angry light grew in intensity behind his eyes and he stood flatfooted. After a few minutes he let his voice cut back through the room: "Hurry up, Lafayette."

The editor gave him a cursory glance and said, "In a minute." Then, after another half-minute of talk with the printer, he came up to the counter and frowned at MacIver. "Now, then. What can I do for you?"

MacIver pulled the folded newspaper from under his arm. It was folded so as to reveal the editorial. Its headline was plain:

WHO HIRED THE KILLER TO WALK OUR STREETS?

MacIver slapped the newspaper down on the counter and suddenly shot his hand forward to grip Lafayette's collar. Lafayette was a foot taller than MacIver but he didn't let that bother him. He jerked the editor forward and laid his grim stare against the editor's eyes; and said, "Who put you up to this, Price?"

Lafayette was ruffled. He struggled plainly with himself but finally he spoke calmly. "Take your hands off me."

MacIver released him, shoving him disdainfully back. "All right. But answer the question."

"Nobody put me up to anything. Did you ever hear of freedom of the press, MacIver? I'm at liberty to express my own opinions on the editorial page of my newspaper. If you disagree that's your privilege. But it gives you no rights to break in here and manhandle me. Now calm down—if you've got a grievance, then express yourself."

MacIver calmed himself with some effort. He pointed at the editorial. "That's a clear attempt to smear Ethan Scott. What do you want to do, crucify him?"

"Are you a friend of Scott's?"

"Yes."

"Then I pity you."

"Never mind the pious clichés, Price. But I remember a day not long ago when you told me you were in favor of hiring Scott. Now you print this. All the time you've published in this town you've been sitting on the fence, sticking a tentative foot out on one side or the other from time to time. But I think this deserves an explanation."

"All right," Lafayette said. "If you want me to spell it out, I will—though my meaning seems clear enough in that editorial, if you bothered to read beyond the headline."

"I read it."

"Then perhaps you noticed that the editorial isn't aimed at Scott. It's aimed at the men who hired him."

"You were in favor of hiring him not long ago."

"That was before I'd seen him," Lafayette said. "It was before I'd seen his methods."

MacIver leaned forward against the counter, painting a synthetic smile across his sensitive lips. "And just how would you go about dealing with toughs, Price? With mealy-mouthed words?"

"Yesterday," Lafayette said, making a point of ignoring him, "two men rode into Lodestar. They didn't give their names and they didn't say where they'd come from. It didn't take your friend Scott more than ten seconds to make up his mind that they were two of Henry Dierkes's toughs."

"They had it stamped on them like a brand," MacIver said disgustedly. "I had a look at them too, Price. Rawhiders—scum. Did you see them?"

"I saw them. At the coroner's office. They'd walked into the Eldorado Saloon for a drink. Scott came in behind them and just stood by the door. He didn't say anything, he didn't do anything. But the way Scott has of looking at a man is as good as a screaming insult from anyone else. Those damned eyes of his prodded those two into making a try for him—and now both of them are dead."

"It's one way to whittle Henry down to size," MacIver murmured.

"He didn't know those two were Dierkes's men. We still don't know. They could have been innocent drifters passing through."

"Then why did they pull guns on him?"

"You'd want to fight him too if he looked at you that way."

"Hell," MacIver said, "his eyes are built that way, Price. He looks at me that way all the time. If you had the guts to go out and look at him yourself, he'd look at you the same way. He looks at everybody that way."

"Then he's a raving-mad killer," Lafayette said flatly.

"No. You're dead wrong. The only thing dangerous a man can see in Ethan Scott's eyes is the reflection of his own conscience. That's what frightened those toughs—their consciences."

"Hogwash," Lafayette said, in the manner of spitting. "I'll tell you something, MacIver—your friend Scott is gun-crazy. The only time anyone's ever seen him smile is when there's a gun in his hand with flame spurting out the barrel."

"That's a lie."

"Is it?" Lafayette said faintly. "Don't be blinded by hero-worship, MacIver. We both know that Scott's the toughest man in Arizona. Well, what of it? What's so admirable about being tough?"

"Scott didn't ask for this job."

"But he accepted it," the editor retorted.

"Yes, he accepted it!" MacIver was thoroughly angered by now and his voice lifted in pitch. "He accepted it just like he's accepted the same kind of work in other towns—a work he's got to do because nobody else has the guts to do the job. You plead with him to take the job. You offer him a huge salary. You tell him he's free to use any damn methods he chooses, just so he gets rid of the toughs. But then you get a look at some of those methods and all of a sudden you start backpedaling. You're scared all of a sudden to go through with what you started—what *you* started, Price. Scott didn't start it. It's men like you that make men like Scott possible. Hell, you're cowards, all of you. You're vultures!"

Having said that much, and feeling too enraged to stay and listen to any more of the editor's pious bleatings, MacIver wheeled and rammed outside, striding angrily back to Bow Street and across to his own side of the line.

"We've got a bull by the tail, damn it," Murvain said to Sheriff Castillo. "I wish to hell I'd never got into this mess."

"I'm inclined to agree," the sheriff said, not elucidating on his motives. He swung his boots down off the rim of his scarred desk and opened a drawer to fish for a toothpick among the mess of miscellaneous articles gathered there. Out front of the desk, Guy Murvain's thickset body was pushing back and forth, aimlessly circling the small room, his heavy hands behind him. "Hell," Murvain said.

"I'd just as soon let Dierkes take over the whole mountain as make Lodestar into a graveyard—and that's just what Scott's doing. How long has he been here—a month?"

"Almost a month."

"And how many dead men have we buried?"

"Eight," the sheriff said positively. "That don't count Arnie, either. Dierkes buried Arnie himself."

"Every one of them shot by Ethan Scott," Murvain said sourly. "He's got this town in the palm of his hand, Gene, and we can't stop him. He'll kill the man who stands in his way."

"Small correction," the sheriff murmured. "Scott didn't kill all of them. One of MacIver's barkeeps took a shotgun to that knife-thrower in the Nugget, remember?"

"MacIver's painted with the same stripe as Scott," Murvain said flatly. "The only difference is in degree—MacIver's not quite so sure of himself as Scott is. Hell, that man Scott would keep right on if the whole world turned against him. It wouldn't mean a damn thing to him, because he figures what's right is what's right for Ethan Scott. Nobody else matters to him. Hell, Gene—we'd be better off without both of them. A whole lot better off."

"Sure," the sheriff said mildly. "But how do you propose to get rid of them?"

"I don't know, damn it. But the way may come. I have the feeling Scott's going to overstep the line sooner or later. Right now the town's not mad enough. Public opinion says he's a thorn in our side, but that's about all. He's doing what he was hired to do—whittle down the toughs. And he's stayed within the letter of the law so far, just as he said he would. But a good many of the men he's killed may or may not have been part of Dierkes's gang. Scott glimpses a tough-looking man and he makes an assumption, and then he picks a fight with the man with his eyes. But I've got the feeling that one day soon he's going to pick a fight with the wrong man—some innocent man—and then hell will pop. Hell will pop, Gene, mark my words. This town won't stand still for murder, whether it's committed by Ethan Scott or by God Almighty."

"Maybe that's Scott's trouble," the sheriff observed.

"He thinks he's God. And with those guns of his, he just about is, I guess."

"Not quite," Murvain said tightly. He stopped his pacing near the door and swung it open to look out. "There he is now, going into the Nugget. Well, it's some small blessing that he's made his headquarters over there instead of on this side of the line. At least we don't have to live with him."

"You ain't that well insulated," the sheriff murmured. "It ain't the other end of the world, over there on the far side of Bow Street. It was on this side of the street he shot Tom Larrabee's elbow to pieces, remember."

"I remember," Murvain said. He sounded sour. "Larrabee's arm will be in that cast from now till doomsday. He may never use his hand again."

"He asked for it," the sheriff said.

"Maybe."

"No. He did. Scott's an arrogant son of a bitch but he ain't a liar. I never heard of him shootin' a man who didn't draw a gun on him first. I suspect the story he told about Larrabee trying to backshoot MacIver was the truth."

"What if it was? Are you so fond of MacIver?"

"No," the sheriff said. "But I don't like to see anybody shot in the back."

Murvain grunted and swung to watch the sheriff pick his teeth. Murvain said, "Well, at least Scott's accomplished something. We've all been able to deliver our payrolls this past week."

"That's what you hired him for, ain't it?"

"Partly. But it doesn't make me like him any the more for it." Murvain clapped his hat on, gave the sheriff one more glum look, and went outside.

The sheriff took the time to finish picking his teeth. Then he stood up and went out into the morning sun. It was, he judged, about eight-thirty. He cast a half-malignant glance in the direction of MacIver's Nugget Saloon, then turned upstreet and quartered across in front of the National Hotel to the livery stable. "Riding out for a look around," he told the hostler, and when his horse was saddled, he swung his overweight mass onto the Texas-rigged hull and dipped his head to clear the top of the wide-mouth doorway, riding out of the stable and around the side of the church and eastward toward the foothills of the Yellows.

Certain suspicions had been tugging at his mind for some time now and this morning he resolved to have them out with Henry Dierkes. *I am nobody's flunky,* he thought resolutely, and put the big bay gelding into the first of the winding canyons and humping crosshills that climbed steadily into the higher reaches of the mountains. His chosen trail lifted him across scrub-covered hilltops and for a while he took the Mountain King mine road until he achieved the top of a pass between the shoulders of a mountain saddle blanketed with catclaw and spindly yucca stalks and scattered boulders; here he turned off the road to the southeast and followed a faintly defined game trail a mile through a tilted boulder field to the fringe of scrub timber at the base of Hutch Peak, which was a lesser mountain leading up into the tortuously rugged chain of the Yellows. He dipped into the trough of a narrow gorge, forded a creek running thin, and rode up the far side of the gorge onto the brief plateau at the far end of which was Henry Dierkes's cabin.

But he raised no one in Dierkes's yard, and a short inspection convinced him that the run-down place was deserted—which meant Dierkes was probably up in his crew's stronghold at Peacock Gorge.

The sheriff removed his big hat and wiped oily sweat from his forehead, and carefully weighed the mounting heat of the day and the discomfort of an additional two-hour ride to Peacock Gorge against his resolution to have things out with Henry Dierkes. At last he sighed, spoke a few pointed Spanish words, and climbed on his horse again, pointing it east toward the Gorge.

It was past ten o'clock now; it would be around noon by the time he reached Dierkes. He resigned himself and settled his fat buttocks back in the saddle, letting the horse jog along at an easy, steady gait. He crossed the road that led up to the Crystal mine, the highest of the mountain mines, and then the trail dropped him onto the floor of a steep-walled canyon with rising yellow limestone cliffs on either side that narrowed his view of the sky and restricted the world; his horse climbed to the head of the long canyon and then entered deeper timber, tall-trunked lodgepole pines and aspen at the seven-thousand-foot level. A carpet of needles and cones covered the ground, muffling the footfalls of the gelding. A creek rushed headlong downslope, dampening him with its spray, and he watered the horse there before continuing upward. A hawk swept along on air currents above, not beating its wings. Climbing to this altitude thinned the air and reduced the temperature by twenty degrees. The sun was only occasionally visible through matted branches overhead.

Peacock Gorge was bounded on two sides by steep talus slopes covered with treacherous shifting shale. The top end of the Gorge was blocked by a marble-like wall, pale white and glowing, and the only access to the Gorge was at its mouth. This was effectively narrowed by boulder outcrops to either side, so that a few men posted in strategic defensive positions could hold off any intended body of attackers indefinitely. Within the Gorge, Peacock Creek ran gurgling down the center from a spring in the granite, and among the pines were scattered the buildings that had been thrown up when the earlier residents had thought the gold vein was a deep one. It had not been. Within two months the vein had petered out and the town had been deserted, and had died. But a good number of log structures remained; and this was where the greatest part of Henry Dierkes's army of toughs lived.

The sheriff made no effort to conceal himself. The only precautionary measure he took was to remove his badge and pocket it. When he rode between the boulder outcrops guarding the mouth of the Gorge, he knew he had been observed, and he rode slowly, so as to give the watchers time to announce his arrival to Dierkes.

He rode in among the trees and off-horsed in front of the covered porch of what had once been the town's saloon. He left the gelding with its reins trailing and stopped below the porch, waiting.

Presently—and it occurred to the sheriff that the man was taking his own sweet time—Dierkes came out to stand on the porch with his arms akimbo. "What you want, Sheriff?"

"Talk," the sheriff said, and climbed the three steps to the porch. He went straight across the boards and into the

barroom. Half a dozen men looked up simultaneously and
fixed him with stares of evident distrust. He heard the
thud of boots behind him and then from the door came
Henry Dierkes's voice: "Clear out, boys."

The toughs showed their plain dislike when they filed
past. Then they were gone, and Dierkes came around in
front of the sheriff, moving his lank, redheaded figure past
the end of the bar and up behind it. "A drink?"

"I don't mind," the sheriff said. He crossed the length
of the room to a table in the back and sat down facing the
door. Dierkes stooped, reaching under the bar for a bottle
and glasses, and brought them back to the table. Dierkes
looked at the sheriff, waiting in an uncertain and wary
manner, and Dierkes chuckled. "Tryin' to make like Ethan
Scott, putting your back to the wall?"

"I just don't trust those low-heeled hairpins you keep
around here for pets."

Dierkes's smile widened. "You're safe enough. What's
on your mind?"

"I don't like being played for a fool," the sheriff said
bluntly.

"All right. What's that supposed to mean?"

"I want to know just what I'm in," the sheriff said. He
waited for Dierkes to fill the two glasses with whiskey.
Then he lifted his, ignored Dierkes's sardonic toast, and
took a swallow. "You ain't in this alone," he said. "I want to
know who it is that's running this show."

"I am," Dierkes said immediately.

"No. Someone's backing your play. I want to know
who."

"Why? What difference does it make?"

"It might make a lot. I want to know, Henry."

"Don't threaten me," Dierkes said. His tone was flat.
But then he smiled again. "What gives you the idea I'm in
this with anybody?"

"A lot of things."

"Such as?"

"Such as, why is it you're so set on getting the payroll
insurance cancelled? Why should you care whether you're
getting the insurance company's money or the mine's?"

"Maybe I don't like bigshot mine owners."

"Sure. You hate them so much you want to drive them out of business, so you can dry up your own source of loot." The sheriff turned his heavy glare directly on Dierkes. "Don't give me that."

Dierkes remained unstirred. "You can think anything you want. Your opinions are on your own time, strictly. But don't expect me to own up to anything."

"Why shouldn't I? I'm in this as deep as you—I got a right to know what's going on, don't I?"

"No."

"And just why the hell don't I?"

"Because I don't trust you."

Heat rose to the sheriff's face. "Maybe you better explain that."

"Glad to," Dierkes said. He took a sip of his drink and set it down, and leaned back with his arms hooked over the back of the chair. "Let's just suppose what you say is true, about somebody backin' my activities. Mind you, I'm admittin' no such thing, but we'll suppose it's true for the sake of argument."

"I'm willing to suppose," the sheriff said caustically.

"Sure you are. Well, if it's true, then only two people know about it—me and the fellow behind me. You don't think I'd let the rest of these stupid gunsels know, do you?"

"I ain't worried about them. I'm thinking about me."

"Yeah," Dierkes said drily. "Suppose I told somebody who it is that's backing me. Suppose that somebody got in a pinch and squealed. Or suppose he decided to blackmail the fellow behind me."

"I ain't about to do either of those things," the sheriff said. "I'm in this as deep as he is. If I was to open my mouth I'd get knocked down right along with him."

"I'm glad you feel that way," Dierkes said.

"Then what's wrong with telling me?"

"Let's just say I gave my word."

"Who to? The man backing you up?"

"If there is such a gent." Dierkes grinned, enjoying this.

"Judas," the sheriff said disgustedly. He emptied his

glass and leaned over it moodily. "How long do you expect me to keep working in the dark?"

"As long as you want to stay around Lodestar," Dierkes said, and added gently, "alive."

"Judas," the sheriff said again, standing up angrily. "I don't know how long I'll put up with it," he told Dierkes, and half-turned toward the door. Sight of a man there arrested him—Raven, with his clawlike hand suspended near his gun. Raven's face was gaunt and cheerless. He said, "He ain't much more use to us, is he?"

"Leave him be," Dierkes said.

Raven gave the sheriff an ugly look that chilled him through; then the gaunt gunman stooped over and coughed harshly, spattering the floor with droplets of blood; and wheeled outside to the porch. The sheriff watched the blood on the floor and said, "He'll be dead inside of six months."

"He knows it," Dierkes said.

"Remember what I said," the sheriff muttered. "Maybe you'll decide to change your mind about telling me."

"I'll remember," Dierkes said, not moving from his chair.

XI

THAT SAME AFTERNOON about three-thirty MacIver was standing by the bar in the Nugget when Marla Searles stood up from Ethan Scott's table and walked toward the door in her riding clothes. MacIver put out a hand, halting her. "I wish you'd carry something bigger than that popgun."

"I'm all right," she said tonelessly, and went on out. MacIver cast a troubled glance over at Scott, whose eyes were on his solitaire game; and after a moment, quietly disturbed by certain things he had seen in the past few weeks, MacIver walked to Scott's table and sat down.

Scott said, without looking up, "Something's bothering you."

"It shows, does it?"

"It shows."

"I don't have as good a poker face as you do," MacIver said drily.

"I know. That's why it's always surprised me a little that you're such a successful gambler."

"Maybe. That isn't what I want to talk about."

"I know," Scott said. "You want to talk about Marla."

MacIver's eyebrows lifted and Scott said, "You're troubled by what you see, or what you think you see, between me and Marla. You want to tell me that the only thing that can possibly happen to her if she tags along after me is that she'll get hurt. You want to ask me for her good to stay away from her."

"I," MacIver said, "will be damned."

Scott nodded. "Very possibly. You're not in love with her, are you?"

"No."

"Then this is just friendly interest."

"Yes."

"Then all I can tell you is this. I'm sure if she knew of it she'd appreciate your concern, but she's a grown woman and her eyes are wide open. She's made her choice."

"You."

Scott shrugged. "She knows what I am and she knows the end that will come to me."

"You know," MacIver said, "when I first met her she reminded me of you in some ways. Maybe after all I shouldn't stick my nose in."

"I don't mind," Scott said gently.

MacIver nodded slowly and walked back to his office. He sat down and, with no real purpose in mind, pulled out a desk drawer and looked idly inside. A crumpled piece of paper caught his eye and he drew it out, smoothing it flat. It was the note he had received a month ago. It began: "*If you want to know what Marla Searles does all the time when she's out riding....*"

It made him frown with thought, and then, quickly, he stood up, pocketing the note and striding forward on his short legs to the street. He turned north, and saw two things: The sheriff was just ducking his head to ride a lathered horse into the livery stable, and Marla was just riding away in the opposite direction, past the church and east toward the foothills. MacIver wondered idly what the fat sheriff had been doing out riding on a hot day like this; but he presently forgot it and walked upstreet toward the stable. The sheriff was just coming out, and dipped his head in stiff courtesy, grunting, "*Buenos tardes*, MacIver," and walked away down the boardwalk. MacIver entered the stable, found the hostler and rented a horse for the day.

In five minutes he was mounted and leaving town. He cantered eastward, with no more definite plan in mind than to follow Marla and find out where she went. The anonymous note had given him the idea, and he realized he might once again be poking his nose in where it did not belong; but he wasn't as sure of Marla as he was of Ethan Scott, and he thought that just possibly Scott might be in need of a little more protection than he knew.

Atop a low, bald hill he paused to sweep the rising land ahead, and caught a glimpse of a rider a half mile away dipping off a hump of land out of sight. He pointed the rented horse in that direction and gigged it with his heels, trotting forward under the lash of the afternoon sun. He heard the clop of the pony's hoofs and the dry jingle of bit chains; sunlight glinted harshly off the metal parts of the bridle and off flickering mica particles in the ground, and he squinted against the glare. The smell of dust was heavy. This was September on the high desert and the temperatures easily surpassed the hundred-degree mark; he felt sweat roll freely from his forehead and palms and armpits.

He reined in just short of the summit of the hill where he had last caught sight of Marla, and not wishing to give himself away, he dismounted and climbed the rest of the distance to the top on foot to have a look beyond. But no one was in sight in the small valley below, and so he went back to the horse, gathered the reins and mounted, and rode forward once more.

It took twenty minutes to cross the little valley, on the

far side of which he again dismounted below the lip of a hill and climbed up for a look. This time he found riders below—two riders, approaching the tree-lined creek from opposite directions, apparently about to meet, and intentionally so. The nearer rider, with her back to MacIver, was Marla. He couldn't be sure, but the farther horseman looked familiar—he almost thought it might be Henry Dierkes. Frowning, he settled down to wait.

Marla reached the clearing by the stream's edge, dismounted and tied her horse's reins up to the branch of a mesquite. She went forward then and stood in the shade of a thick-bole cottonwood. Not long thereafter hoofbeats telegraphed forward along the ground and Henry Dierkes appeared threading the trees. He stepped down nearby and she could see that very little of his usual cheer was showing on his face. He spoke almost immediately: "Somebody lock you in your room? Somebody break your legs?"

"No," she said quietly.

"This is the first time you've been here in a week. That made a lot of ridin' for me, down here and back every day, just to take a look at any empty clearing."

"Calm down," she told him. She settled her back against the tree and hooked her thumbs in the belt she wore to hold up her little gun.

Dierkes took two steps and halted, frowning down. "What's eatin' you? What's wrong?"

The girl stooped to uproot a long-bladed yellow grass stalk. She began breaking off little segments of it; she said, "I only came today to tell you I won't be coming here any more."

"What? What the hell?"

She lifted her eyes to meet his glance evenly. "It's over, that's all."

"That's all," he said, in a weak tone of disbelief. "Easy to say, ain't it? Now wait just a minute, Marla."

She held up her palm, quieting him. "We had an agreement. Remember?"

"What agreement?"

"That we'd only keep seeing each other as long as it suited our mutual convenience."

"What of it?"

"It's not convenient to me any more," she said. She found another grass stalk and pulled it up.

"Well," he said sarcastically, "ain't that sweet. And that—just where does it leave me?"

"Out in the cold, I'm afraid. But I can't help it."

"Oh," he said. "You can't, can't you?" His glance narrowed with suspicion. "It's that God damned lizard-eyed Ethan Scott, ain't it?"

She didn't answer immediately, and his voice lifted: "Ain't it, Marla?"

"That's not your affair," she told him, and stood away from the tree trunk. "I've said what I came to say."

"Just like that?"

"Just like that. Goodbye, Henry." Saying the last very softly, she turned and walked briskly to her horse, and climbed to the saddle.

Not until then did Dierkes move. He ran his hand down his thigh behind his gun, as if to wipe sweat off his palm, and turned his freckled countenance toward her, saying in a flat and hard way, "I intend to scatter Ethan Scott all over the street of Lodestar in pieces. You can tell him that for me." Dierkes whirled and walked toward his horse with long-legged strides.

Marla sat her saddle watching while he savagely neck-reined his horse around and sank spurs into its flanks and plunged away toward the dark mountains; then, with her face a solemn mask, she turned forward and tapped her heels against her horse's belly.

MacIver caught up with her on the road to town. He drew alongside and rode silently for a moment, watching the grave turn of her face; and presently Marla said, "You followed me."

"Admitted."

"And you're worried."

"Yes."

"You want to know why I met Henry Dierkes."

"Yes, damn it. In case you haven't heard, Marla, I've made it my business to cover Ethan's back for him. That includes whatever you do behind his back."

"I can't tell you what I said to Dierkes," she said, "but I can tell you this: I won't be meeting him again."

Her eyes met his. "That will have to satisfy you, Krayle."

He regarded her stonily. "It will do for the moment. But if I ever again spot you within a hundred feet of Dierkes, that's when my mouth will open."

"That's fair enough," she said; and they rode the remaining distance to Lodestar in silence, each of them troubled with his own thoughts.

They separated at the stable after leaving their horses. Marla turned east, toward the back of town, and MacIver walked down Bow Street to the Nugget. Sight of a particular horse tied up in front of the saloon made him hurry his steps; he thought he recognized that horse. He walked rapidly into the saloon and stopped just inside to sweep the place with his worried glance.

A few customers stood in a tight-packed bunch back at the far end of the bar, trapped there by circumstances and unable to leave; they stood with fright naked on their faces. But that wasn't what kept MacIver's attention. Out in the center of the room, right by the bar, a gaunt man stood coughing with a rasp. The gaunt man faced the table where Ethan Scott sat before his lonely card game; the gaunt man was Raven.

MacIver had no way of knowing how it had started, but that was of little consequence. What was plain enough was that Raven had come in specifically with the intention of picking a fight with Scott. It occurred to MacIver that if Scott was unafraid, Raven was equally unafraid—the tubercular gunman knew he was dying anyway. A stray, odd thought flashed through MacIver's head: *We're all of us dying, aren't we?*

Scott's head moved slightly and he spoke. "Stay out of this Krayle."

MacIver stepped back, drawing Raven's momentary attention, and that instant's distraction gave Scott his chance. MacIver saw the flicker of Scott's hand and then Scott had a gun out trained on Raven. Scott said in a drone, "I don't want to kill you today, Raven. Walk out of here."

Raven coughed consumptively and straightened. "You talk pretty tough when you got the drop on me."

"You know better than that."

"I think I can beat you," Raven said.

"You'd have no chance," Scott answered evenly.

"No, I reckon not—not as long as you hold that gun on me."

"Walk out of here," Scott said.

Coughing racked Raven's body. Blood spurted from his lips, specking the floor. He said, "Damn you," and turned slowly toward the door. He paused then and looked over his shoulder at Scott. "One day before I die I want a chance at you."

"I whipped you once," Scott said. "You still carry the bullet. Isn't that enough?"

"Not enough," Raven said, shaking his head. "Not near enough. You were lucky in Tombstone—but it won't be enough until you're dead, Scott."

Raven pointed himself at the door once more and walked forward unsteadily. MacIver was right in his path and knew Raven wouldn't bother to go around him, so he stepped aside to let Raven pass.

His mistake was in stepping to the left instead of to the right. By moving to his left he put himself between Raven's path and Ethan Scott—and that, he realized too late, was exactly what Raven wanted. MacIver gathered his muscles to jump back but it was no good. Raven's arm locked around his throat from behind and he felt the jab of Raven's gun in his side, pinching his flesh against his ribs. Raven's voice cut across the saloon with force:

"Stand up and holster your gun, Scott—or I'll cut MacIver in half."

Slowly, reluctantly, Scott pushed his chair back and stood up. He pushed his coattail back and let his gun fall loosely into its scabbard. But this was no good either, MacIver realized—now Raven had the drop on Scott; and Raven wouldn't hesitate to use it. MacIver had got Scott into this; he had to get him out. He felt the pressure of the gun lift away from his ribs. Raven must be moving his gun to bear on Scott. And MacIver made his move. He whirled with all his energy, toward the right, toward Raven's gun;

his arm struck the side of Raven's gun, numbing him all the way up to his shoulder, but it knocked the gun aside and unsettled the weak gunman on his feet. MacIver kept turning, making a full revolution past Raven into the clear. He stopped against the bar, facing the center of the room. Once again Ethan Scott had his guns drawn; and when Raven gained his balance, Scott said, "Stalemate, Raven. You've got the choice. Holster your weapon and walk out of here, or try a shot at me. It's up to you."

Raven blinked at him. "I think you're scared." His arm began to rise with the pistol but then a fit of coughing overcame him and he doubled over, closing his eyes.

MacIver saw his opportunity quickly. He leaped forward from the bar, snatched Raven's gun out of the limp hand and stepped back. Raven straightened up, his eyes moist, and MacIver waved the man's own gun at him. "Out."

"No."

That was Scott. Scott came striding forward, his eyes glittering. He crossed the width of the room and stood before MacIver with an undiminished brittle light in his glance. "I told you to stay clear of this," he said tightly, and took the gun from MacIver's hand. Then he turned to Raven. His own guns were holstered and he said, "I gave you two chances to turn away from a fight and you passed them both up. I won't give you another."

Scott reversed Raven's gun in his fist, shot his hand forward and slid the gun into Raven's holster; and stepped back. Watching all this, MacIver felt flustered and a little ashamed.

"Now," Scott said softly, "draw on me."

Raven showed no fear. He coughed once and took a single backward step, bracing his feet; he rubbed his hands together and let his arms fall slowly to his sides. "This is the way I wanted it, Scott."

"Then you've got it."

"I can beat you."

"You can try."

Raven blinked. His hand lifted, catching up his revolver and cocking it as it rose. The muzzle cleared the lip of his holster and then two bullets crashed out of Ethan

cott's big forty-fives into Raven's body. It hurled Raven
back against the bar. He spun and collided with MacIver,
and bounced away and fell flopping to the floor. MacIver
waved his arms to keep from losing his balance; he came to
rest in time to see Scott sliding his guns back into leather.
Scott turned his face and his voice was a hiss:

"Don't ever do that again, Krayle." After which he
left, his coat flapping behind him.

XII

MARLA LOOKED at him with a certain bitterness; Scott said,
"It will come to a head soon now. I've cut down every one
of the men Dierkes kept around him as buffers. He's got
nothing left but that hardscrabble crew of rawhiders up in
the mountains, and he knows he can't depend on them.
And he thinks I've taken you away from him. Altogether,
that's enough to make him come down out of the hills after
me. He's avoided it this long but he won't any longer—
he's got to finish me."

"What do you think he'll do?"

"I can't say. I've got to be ready, that's all."

"You make it sound easy."

"No," he said. "It's never easy."

She turned her face away. "I'd rather not think about
it."

"I'd rather not see you wilt just now," he said with a
slight tinge of dryness. "Marla, I need a favor."

"Go on."

"There's one thing I've got to do before I give Dierkes
his chance at me."

"What is it?"

"You used to be good at imitating handwriting. Can
you get a sample of Henry's?"

"I have a few notes he sent me," she said.

"Good. Get them."

Marla went across her room to the rolltop desk opened it and thumbed through a litter of papers. Finall' she found what she sought and brought back three pen ciled notes, holding them out to him without hesitation.

Scott did not look at them. What he said was, "I wan you to write a note to Tom Larrabee and sign it 'Henry.'"

MacIver hadn't the slightest idea what it was all about, but at Scott's request he went with Scott to the sheriff's office. The sheriff was in, behind his desk with his feet up, and he dropped his legs and came upright in the chair with a little crash when Scott walked in. Scott said, "I need you."

"What for?"

"You and MacIver are going to witness something."

"Witness what?"

Scott turned to MacIver, took a cheroot from MacIver's pocket, put it between his lips and ignited it. He tossed the dead match on the sheriff's desk and said, "It may have occurred to you that there's a man who cracks the whip over Henry Dierkes's ears."

"It's occurred to me," the sheriff said.

Scott's eyebrows moved up a fraction of an inch—a sign of his surprise. "I have reason to suspect the man in question is Tom Larrabee."

The sheriff offered no argument, "And?"

"I've arranged a trap," Scott said. "I've had a note sent to Larrabee, a note in Dierkes's handwriting. It asks Larrabee to meet Dierkes at ten o'clock—just ten minutes from now—in the livery stable across the street from the National Hotel."

"Go on."

"If Larrabee keeps that appointment, it will confirm my suspicions."

"Maybe," the sheriff said. "But it won't be strong enough proof to hold up in court."

"Let that be my concern," Scott told him quietly. "You just come along with us."

It surprised MacIver a little that the sheriff put up no fight. The sheriff only said, "All right," took his hat off the rack by the door and followed them outside.

Lamplighted windows made a patchwork of the town.
Cooler breezes came out of the alleyways, ruffling the
small hairs at the base of MacIver's neck, and he felt a
distinct premonition of grief. He looked both ways along
the street, stopping to examine each pedestrian in sight,
but Tom Larrabee was not visible. MacIver walked with
Scott and the sheriff unhurriedly up Bow Street and across
it to the stable. Inside the arch of the stable door, Scott
spoke to the hostler: "Go on back in the office and shut
yourself in."

The hostler touched his beard. "Trouble?"

"Maybe."

"Just so," the hostler murmured and went back through
a door which closed immediately.

Scott said, "You two post yourselves in that empty
stall. Don't show yourselves."

"Wait a minute," the sheriff said. "I won't stand for an
ambush, señor."

"If I intended to ambush him, would I have invited
you along to watch? Get out of sight, gentlemen, and don't
make noise."

MacIver gave the sheriff a gentle shove and accompa-
nied him back into the dim stall. Out in the wide aisle of
the stable runway, Ethan Scott removed the cigar from his
lips and dropped it. MacIver watched the sole of Scott's
boot crush out the embers. Then Scott went to the wall,
lifted the chimney of the only lamp in the place and
extinguished it, and faded back into the deep shadows
along the runway. MacIver lost sight of him. The open
mouth of the big doorway was gray and indistinct against
the night. Somewhere a dog barked once or twice and
lifted a howl that broke off into a series of descending yips.
Beside MacIver, the sheriff shuffled nervously and MacIver
whispered, "Be quiet."

The sheriff settled down. Horses drummed by on the
street and presently MacIver's eyes became accustomed to
the dimness. A freight wagon creaked past, lifting a slow
cloud of thin dust into the stable, and then MacIver heard
the shuffle of boots in the street outside. In time the tall,
hatless figure of Tom Larrabee stood silhouetted in the
door, one arm in a bent plaster cast. Larrabee advanced

ten feet into the aisle and stood uncertainly. His left hand went to a pocket and produced a match, which he flicked alight on his thumbnail and held up above his head while he squinted, peering into the dark. "Henry? It's me—what the hell do you want?"

"I want you," Ethan Scott said, walking forward from the shadows.

The match fell from Larrabee's upraised hand. It coursed through a short arc and went out before it hit the ground. There was still enough light from the doorway for MacIver to see the two men in silhouette. Scott said, "You walked into it, Larrabee, I'm sorry to say. I sent that note."

Larrabee stiffened. "So?"

"It establishes that you're on Henry Dierkes's side of the fence."

"Why should it? I got a note and came up here because I wanted to find out what it was all about."

"No," Scott said. "That's not good enough."

"Then put me on trial and see how much you can prove!"

"You are on trial," Scott droned. "I've heard the evidence and brought in a verdict. I've passed sentence on you, Larrabee."

"The hell!" After that quick ejaculation, Larrabee turned so that his left side was toward Scott. He stood with his head bent and MacIver thought he must be frowning; and then, suddenly, Larrabee's head lifted. "All right. Henry's working for me. Is that what you wanted to know?"

"I already knew it."

"Now what do you do? I haven't got a gun. You can see that."

"Can I?"

Larrabee stood perfectly still; he said softly, "I guess not, my friend."

That was when MacIver saw flame burst out of the tip of the cast on Larrabee's arm. The muffled crack of a small-bore gunshot reached MacIver's ears and on the heels of it Scott's two guns opened up, fired a shot apiece and quit. Larrabee leaned forward. His cast spurted flame

into the ground and he fell, rolling on his side. His leg
twitched; he lay motionless.

"*Jesus Cristo!*" the sheriff said.

Scott was by the wall, holding a lighted match to the
lamp. He turned up the wick, walked forward and crouched
by Larrabee's prone figure. One gun appeared in Scott's
fist and chopped down sharply, smashing the blunt end of
the cast on Larrabee's arm, and then Scott reached down
to pick up a small metal object. He stood up and handed it
to the sheriff. "He's been walking around for a month with
this in his hand. The cast was much bigger than it had to
be—that was easy to see. But he forgot one thing."

"What?"

"It's not as easy to aim a cast as it is to aim a gun,"
Scott said. His dismal gray eyes locked with the sheriff's.
"I trust when this story's told, the whole truth will be
told."

"I've got no reason to lie about it," the sheriff said,
and knelt beside the body.

Scott turned his chipped-rock stare to MacIver. "Come
on."

Filled with the backwash of astonishment, MacIver
stumbled through the door and went numbly down the
street beside Scott's slow-moving figure. One at a time,
Scott lifted his guns and punched out the empty shell
case, and reloaded the chamber. Scott said, "The play's
almost over. It's the last act and there are only two scenes
left."

"What are they?"

"Henry Dierkes," Scott breathed. "Henry's the first
scene. After that the final scene will show us Murvain and
the vultures taking over. They'll get a new broom and
sweep the streets clean from one end of the town to the
other. You and I are part of the trash they'll throw out.
When the curtain comes down, you and I won't be on
stage any more."

"Then I guess it's about time for us to pull out,"
MacIver said.

"Not yet, not for me. I've got to wait for Henry."

"In God's name why?"

Scott shook his head. "I take no pleasure in what

people think of me, or in how much money I'm paid, or in how many shots I fire. But if I'm going to justify my life, Krayle, I've got to finish the jobs I start—I've got to carry my own cross. But the roof is about to cave in, and when Henry's back is broken it will all fall down. You'd be smart to sell out now."

MacIver almost brought up his habitual objection, but he didn't. He had already seen most of the fun, and it hadn't been fun. And so he said, "I think perhaps you're right. But one day I'd like to still be around when the vultures burn their own town down around their ears."

"It will never happen that way. The vultures always win."

"Must they?"

Scott didn't answer him; he only said, "Sell out, Krayle."

"I guess," MacIver said. He left Scott at the door of the Nugget and continued south along Bow Street, crossing over near the foot of the street to Nita Matlock's café. Nita was just closing the place; he waited for her to put the key in her bag, then took her arm and walked her toward home. She looked at him; moonlight washed her face smoothly and she said, "You're quiet tonight."

"I'm leaving Lodestar," he said. "Selling my place."

He heard the swiftness of her indrawn breath. "Why, Krayle?"

"Lodestar's about to take a bath, in blood. I've had enough. If I don't leave voluntarily, I'll probably be kicked out by the good citizenry. They don't want my kind around anymore."

"I don't see anything wrong with your kind."

He stopped, halting her, and turned, lifting her chin with his forefinger. "You're a sweet woman, Nita. When I leave I'll ask you to come with me. Will you?"

"Where?"

"There's been a new strike over at Harshaw," he said. "I thought I might try my luck there."

He watched her head bob down; she smiled, because it was good to smile, and she said, "I'll come."

His usual hour for arising was ten o'clock, but this morning he was up before eight. He bathed, shaved and dressed meticulously according to habit, heated up yesterday's remaining coffee and made a breakfast of that, and was in his office behind the Nugget before nine. There was a good deal of work to be done this morning and he removed his coat, hung it over his chair and took off his shoulder-rigged gun, which he put on top of the safe. His tie he draped over the coat; he loosened his shirt collar and found himself unable to shake the feeling of anxious pressure that had been troubling him since awakening. *It's the last day,* he thought. But why? He could not answer himself. *The last day.* He knew it; it was like a cooler current of knowledge coming out of the shadows, its origin somewhere in obscurity.

He sat down and began pulling out drawers. One by one he emptied them. What he did not want he threw in a careless pile in the room's back corner; what he intended to keep—and this was very little—he put on top of the desk. Presently the desk was cleaned out, and what remained on top of it was a small sheaf of assorted documents, most of them IOU's from customers that he knew he would never collect on. These he set aside in a separate stack and tied with string. The rest of the papers were small bills of sale and odd jotted notes that would have pressed him hard to explain their value. They were, in the main, memories.

This much done he turned to the safe, spun the dial and swung the door back. Inside were the cashbox, a file of partnership agreements and deeds, and a pile of assorted business papers. He opened the cashbox and took the time to count its contents. When he subtracted from that the amount it would take to pay off his help and pay existing debts, he still had over five thousand dollars remaining in loose cash, and that would be ample. He would be able to accept bank drafts for the sale of his properties.

He was turning back toward the safe when knuckles rapped the door and he lifted his face. "Come in."

The visitor was Sheriff Eugenio Castillo. The fat man walked in and closed the door behind him and stayed there, leaning back against the door. "So it's true."

"What's true?"

"You really are leaving."

"Who told you that?"

"Nita Matlock mentioned it to me at breakfast. She's selling out too." The sheriff looked around a trifle uncomfortably. "Mind if I sit down?"

"Suit yourself," MacIver said with some reserve.

The sheriff sat. He was sweating heavily; he pulled out a crumpled bandanna to mop his face. "The members of the combine are all set to explode."

"About Larrabee?"

The sheriff nodded; his chins wobbled. "Murvain wants me to arrest Ethan Scott."

"What for?"

"I don't think Murvain was convinced by the story I told him."

"What did you tell him?"

"The truth," the sheriff said, and grunted. "Only the truth. I told him Larrabee admitted he was behind the payroll holdups. Murvain didn't believe me. I told him about the gun in Larrabee's cast, and he didn't believe that either until I showed him the outline of the gun in the fragments of the cast. Then I told him Larrabee shot first, and he just looked at me, as if to say 'So what?'"

"What kind of blood does Murvain want?"

"I wish I knew. He told me to arrest Scott. I told him to arrest him himself. Murvain has been aching to tear Scott limb from limb ever since Scott stood up to him and talked him down."

MacIver nodded. "Why tell me all this?"

"I thought Scott might like to know they're after his blood."

"Why not tell Scott?"

"He don't think much of me," the sheriff said drily. Then he turned serious. "But then, I guess he hasn't got much reason to like me, eh?"

"Am I supposed to consider that a confession that you've been working with Dierkes?"

"I would not go quite that far," the sheriff said cautiously, lapsing into his accent. "On the other hand, señor, you notice I deny nothing. You will have to make what you want of it."

The sheriff found a toothpick in the pocket of his vest and used it to clean his teeth while he talked. His voice came out distorted around the toothpick. "Let us just say I have not lost sight of which side the butter is on. I don't think it is on Henry's side any more."

"Meaning?"

"Meaning I think it's about time for me to pack my gear and clear out of here while I can. I've had a good look at your friend Scott—and I do not believe Henry can cut it. I really don't. But even if he did he would be washed up in this part of the country. The people are angry too much. No matter what happens with Scott these people will not stand for Henry any more. If Scott doesn't kill him the town will—and I don't wish to get caught in the sluice with him."

The sheriff put his toothpick away and stood up, putting his hat on. "So I am leaving. Perhaps I was never much good, but one thing I've got is a good healthy respect for my own skin. I want to keep it, you see? You're a good man, MacIver, and I am glad to see you get out too, while you can." The sheriff nodded briskly for emphasis, turned his broad back and went.

MacIver watched the door thoughtfully for a few moments, wondering just what had prompted the sheriff to talk to him; presently he shrugged it off and turned back to the safe to remove the several partnership agreements and deeds. These he pocketed. Then he went to the closet and brought out its sole contents, a fat leather satchel, creased and marked with the years. He opened this and put into it everything from his desk and the safe that he wished to keep. Everything else went into the discard pile in the corner. He put the half-full satchel away in the safe, locked it up and put on his coat before going out into the barroom.

In early today, Ethan Scott was sitting at his customary table by the west wall, and he had company—Marla. MacIver turned that way, touched his hatbrim in greeting and stopped by the table to speak to Marla: "I thought I'd offer this to you first, though you probably won't want it. Do you want to buy out my interest in the Nugget?"

Marla's coolly beautiful face regarded Ethan Scott for

a measured interval. Scott's expression did not break and he did not speak; he gave no visible signal. Marla said to MacIver, "No. But thanks just the same, Krayle."

"Then you may have a new partner soon," he said. "I'll sell to someone."

She looked at Scott once more; "That's right," she murmured, "I may have a new partner."

MacIver's glance moved to Scott. "The sheriff just left my office."

"I saw him," Scott said.

"He wanted me to relay a message to you. He said Murvain is getting hotter under the collar by the minute, about Larrabee."

"That's to be expected."

MacIver nodded. He said, "The sheriff's pulling up stakes."

"Smart."

MacIver shrugged and turned, and left them.

His first stop was at Turk Chaffee's narrow saloon across the street. No one was in the place except one bartender, whom MacIver asked where Chaffee might be found.

The bartender used his thumb to indicate the office door, at the side of the narrow room, and MacIver crossed the floor to it and knocked.

When Chaffee called out he entered the room and said, "Morning Turk."

"Mac. What can I do for you?"

"I won't beat around the bush," MacIver said. "You've had your eye on the Nugget for a long time. Do you want to buy it?"

"That depends on what you want for it."

"I only own a two-thirds interest in it."

Chaffee said, "Oh? Who's got the rest?"

"Marla."

"I see," Chaffee said, and considered it. "Well, I've got nothing against her, God knows. What do you want for your two-thirds?"

"What's it worth to you?"

Chaffee sat back and rubbed his chin. "I hadn't thought about it, you know."

"Think about it now."

"You're in a hurry?"

"Maybe."

Chaffee's eyebrows went up. "Leaving town?"

"Yes."

"Oh," Chaffee said. "On account of Scott."

"Not really. I'd have pulled out sooner or later anyway. I always do—I'm a fiddlefoot."

"I guess we've got that in our blood, you and me," Chaffee observed. "Well, I'd say as a rough guess, the Nugget with all its fixtures is worth maybe fifty thousand. How's that strike you?"

The place was worth more than that, and MacIver knew it as well as Chaffee, but what he said was, "I'd rather not take the time to look for offers all over town. Let's say my two-thirds interest is worth sixty-thousand and we'll settle it."

Chaffee displayed surprise. "I figured you for more of a horse trader."

"I am when I've got the time."

"Well, we both know for a fact the place is worth more than that, but I'll make you out a draft right now if you're willing."

"Done," MacIver said. "I've got the deed right here."

XIII

THE TOWN, big as it was, still blended in a fading way into the desert plain's common weathered gray-tan. Heat and loose hazy dust lay close along the broad, bright surface of Bow Street; a scatter of horses stood around, hipshot and half asleep on their feet, their tails flicking away flies now and then. There was a quietly threatening loneliness on the almost deserted street. For a single moment, not a sound broke the stillness, and that moment stood like a broken instant of time, stretching. Then two cowboys rounded the corner before the Nugget, stirring up dust and sound, and dismounted to walk inside, leaving behind the smell of saddle sweat. The brass sun of this hot afternoon glared harshly against windows and particles of dust. Scott tarried briefly on the Nugget porch, then went inside and walked with slow strides to his table. His solitaire game was laid out, half finished from when he had left it half an hour ago. He sat, removed his hat, placed one revolver on the table within quick reach, and put his attention on the game.

Marla Searles came forward from somewhere back in the room and stood across the table from him; and when he looked up, she pulled a chair back and sat. She held her lips together in speculative fullness. Sunlight, cutting through the window, rippled along the gloss of her hair.

Scott's eyes were grave; his clipped words rode on a flat voice. "What is it?"

"You," she said. Her glance shuttled around the saloon. No one was nearby. What few customers were in the place stood against the bar across the room. The Nugget, with Ethan Scott posted here, was no longer a popular gathering place, except for those curious newcomers to Lodestar who came for a look at the legend sitting behind his lonely card table.

Marla said, "You make me feel like a woman—and sometimes it frightens me."

"Why?"

Her eyelids were close. "It's clouding up—perhaps it will rain."

"Go on," he said.

Her shoulders swayed a little. "I don't like to be frightened. My mind knows what will come of you. I think too clearly that way. And still I don't want to lose you. Does that sound childish?"

"No." Scott rolled a cigar between his fingers and looked up with a half-shuttered gaze. Some brief emotion stirred his lips, and went away. He said, "I can do nothing that will make it easier for you."

"No," she said faintly, "I don't suppose you can."

The murmur of distant subdued conversations reached them from the far side of the room. Two or three men were watching Scott in the mirrors, curious or indignant or full of awe. Scott knew of that appraisal but he paid it no attention. He might have been alone in the room with the woman. The intensity of the light suddenly diminished at the window when a cloud crossed the sun; Scott spoke in a voice so low that his words barely traveled as far as the girl: "I didn't make the rules, Marla. But I've had to learn them."

It seemed to say something new to her, something she had not considered before. She looked at the gun lying by his fist. The blunt shiny noses of bullets were visible in the open fronts of the cylinder chambers. She said, "That's your life."

"What?"

"That gun," she said, "it's your life—and now you hate it, don't you?"

"I can't say," he muttered. His glance moved deliberately away. At the back end of the bar stood five or six of the girls who worked in the Nugget. Now a group of miners was walking back toward them and the professor, seeing this movement, turned toward the keyboard and began tinkling a tune on the piano. The girls and miners moved onto the dusted floor; the miners danced, in grim fury, with the rouged women, and the echo of the calculated laughter was brittle.

Scott said, "You're the only woman in my life who hasn't tried to change me."

"Perhaps I'd like you to change."

He shook his head briefly. "You want me as I am."

"Not really. But I never saw a woman live happily with the changes she put in a man. A man hates a woman who makes him change."

He touched the gun; he pulled his hand back. "I've never meant to bind myself to anyone. You know that, don't you?"

"I won't hang on you."

"No," he said, "you'd never do that."

The crowd grew slowly; the room became louder and warmer and the heavy thickness of smoke and liquor smells and men's voices droning rolled hard against him, while outside above Lodestar the deep clouds crawled westward from the heights of the Yellows, bringing rain.

Marla's glance dropped to her hands and a faraway resignation took hold of her face; she became at once smaller and heavier, with a gently grave expression, and she said, "I don't suppose there's really any answer for us."

"No."

Her face moved, so that it was cocked, just a little to the side, and she said to him, "If it weren't for that gun—"

"The gun," he answered, "has made me what I am. It giveth and it taketh away. I shall have no regrets."

"No," she breathed, a little sadly, "no regrets."

Scott stood up, sweeping the room with his hard and guarded glance, and moved slowly across the saloon. The bar was crowded now. He drove his shoulder between two men, making a place for himself, and asked for a drink. His face was blank; his eyes glowed expressionlessly as always but in him just now was an immense force of breakage.

Gravel reported the crush of many boots, and on that signal Henry Dierkes rose from his table in the empty Peacock Gorge saloon. The ceiling sagged a bit near one corner of the room; some of the floorboards were rotted and split. Dierkes's eyes were glazed and bitter to a depth. He settled his guns at his hips, with a sort of finality of motion, and lifted his oilskin slicker off the back of the chair. He found the hole in the center of the slicker and put his head through it, letting the slicker fall around him. Then he turned and walked steadily to the door and through it to the porch.

Moving like a mechanism, he stooped to lock the door behind him and dropped the key forgotten in the musty dirt of the shadowed porch boards. He put his back to the door, looking out past the porch through the slashing downpour at the gray shapes and gray faces of the eighteen men gathered dripping before him. They were all that was left of his crew, these eighteen pinch-lipped men of the back trails. The others had, each of them, seen in some nebulous way the collapse of whatever promise had kept them here; and quietly, saying nothing, they had drifted

away one by one. Dierkes knew their kind too intimately
to think of blaming them; he was in a way a fatalist and had
little contempt for men of a kind of which he was one, men
who only lacked some of the final courage he possessed.
He felt a small pity for these eighteen before him who had
chosen to stay. They too were on the wane, and so was he,
but they were too dogged to quit. Habit was too strong a
pattern.

A single horseman threaded the crowd and rode up to
the edge of the porch, sitting his saddle stiffly in the rain.
This was an immensely tall man wearing a round derby
hat, a newcomer; he said, "Hello, Dierkes."

"Evenin', San Saba," Dierkes said, in a voice indiffer-
ent as the derby-hatted man's.

"I see I ain't late," San Saba said. "I rode all night."

"You're in time," said Dierkes. From his pocket he
lifted a heavy canvas sack, which he pushed out from
under his slicker and handed to San Saba. "Two thousand
in gold. That's what you asked."

"All right," San Saba said, and put the gold poke in
his saddlebag. "It's Ethan Scott, ain't it?"

"Yes."

"That's what the gold is buyin'."

San Saba looked around at the stubbled men bunched
up by the porch. A vast contempt rose in his glance and he
said, "I'll wait down at the mouth of the gorge." He reined
his horse gently around and drove it through the crowd,
back the way he had come; and quickly disappeared into
the curtain of rain.

"No need for a speech," Dierkes said to his men.
"Saddle up."

They milled back, not talking at all, and scattered into
the shadows. Dierkes stood on the porch then, in no
hurry, motionless with his quiet memories. He viewed the
sodden ground and the miserable dark rain without really
seeing it. His skin was colored of old copper, flaked with
darker spots. "The last day," he said aloud, with no one
around to hear; "The last day, and it's been fun, boys."

The air was thick and soggy with compressing moisture. A dreary resignation overcame him and was broken
for a brief instant by a feeling that lifted his heart, the

anticipation of the kind of frenzied action that he lived for; then his eyes fell to his hands, noticing their slight tremor, and his glance turned dark once more. His tone was reluctant and drily sharp: "Marla—I'll see him in hell. Well, then, it has been fun."

He tossed his head back as if to look at the sky, but overhead was the porch roof that was impenetrably black. He stood that way, softly singing:

> Now up the rope I go, up I go.
> Well, up the rope I go, up I go.
> And those bastards down below,
> They're saying, "Sam, we told you so,"
> They're saying, "Sam, we told you so,"
> God damn their eyes.

His head dropped until his chin lay against his chest; and he sang the last verse:

> But now in Heaven I dwell, in Heaven I dwell.
> Yes, now in Heaven I dwell, in Heaven I dwell;
> Yes, now in Heaven I dwell,
> And I've been here for a spell,
> And all those bums are down in Hell,
> God damn their eyes.

His voice trailed off and he stood fast; he stood that way a full five minutes, his head down, before he performed his last act as the boss of Peacock Gorge.

In a way it was an admission. He took down the lamp from beside the door, removed its chimney and pulled the stopper from the oil tank. He waved the lamp up and down, splashing coal oil around on the splintered boards and logs, and then, after only a brief hesitation, he lit a match and tossed it on the oil.

Flames burst high and yellow. Dierkes stepped off the porch, not looking back, striding down past the trees to get his horse. He hummed softly the melody of "Sam Hall."

Hardly overjoyed, but nonetheless satisfied with his dealings, MacIver walked toward the Nugget at sundown

ith bank drafts in his pocket in place of the deeds and
artnership agreements that had been there earlier in the
ay. It had been a long day's toiling, selling off his proper-
es and interests, and he had not realized three-quarters
ne sum he would have gained had he spent more time
nd attention. But there was enough; MacIver was not a
reedy man. A dark drizzle was beginning to filter down
ut of the overcast sky. Over the Yellows the sky was solid
lack. He reached the corner of Fourth and Bow and
irned north along Bow and at that moment sight of a
1ass of people arrested him.

On the porch of the Nugget, clearly visible above the
eads of the men and women crowding the street, stood
wo tall men facing each other: Guy Murvain and Ethan
cott. They stood surrounded by hundreds of men, filling
he street and the walks, sitting on balconies and standing
n wagon seats and pressing through open doors and
vindows. Guns flourished occasionally—here and there a
lue barrel glinted. A prolonged roar of defiance lifted and
iung in the air.

"Just so," MacIver muttered. "The vultures have found
heir wings."

Apparently, up on the Nugget porch, Guy Murvain
iad just finished making a speech. The crowd shifted and
nilled. Now and then a sudden commotion rippled. *Not a
;roup of men*, MacIver thought. *A crowd is an animal.
`hey smell smoke—they smell blood*.

Tonight the animal was crying out against Ethan
Scott. MacIver heard the beast growling in the streets and
t boosted him forward on his short legs, angrily. At the
Nugget, Guy Murvain stood showing his teeth in rage.
Black clouds collected overhead and MacIver walked alone,
ull of bitterness, ramming through the mass of bodies
vith his fists and elbows and shoulders and even the kick
f his feet. He felt their ascending hostility and it turned
iim sour; he struck back at them more violently than he
iad to in order to make a path. They shouted and struck
oack and cursed him but they let him through. Cold rain
truck his face. He broke through the crowd's inner ring
ind found himself immediately below the Nugget porch,
ind he stopped.

The only two men on the porch were Murvain and Scott, but the crowd pressed close. MacIver could feel its warm collective breath. Guy Murvain stood fixed on a spot, bold malice in his feverishly aroused gaze. He was talking:

"We've had enough, Scott. Don't you see it? Look at them out there—do you think they came to cheer for me? They've seen too much, Scott, too much of you and your kind of savagery! You crossed the line when you killed Tom Larrabee, and every man in this street knows it. Larrabee deserved a trial, not a bullet. They don't want your kind of justice anymore—they're sick of you, Scott—can't you see it, man?"

A vague expression crossed the still face of the gunfighter; and when he spoke he did not lift his voice.

"I can see it. I can see they've finally gathered enough strength to take their town back from me. That's as it has to be, Murvain—and I'll leave Lodestar soon."

"Soon isn't enough."

"It will have to be. I haven't finished the job I was paid to do."

"You've got your ten-thousand-dollar bonus in your pocket, Scott—isn't it enough? Can't you just ride away now? Damn you, if you don't they'll crawl up on this porch and bury you!"

Scott made no answer of any kind. He did not have to. A stillness had settled over the crowd and heads had turned in mass, away from the Nugget porch, toward the south, toward the foot of Bow Street, toward the distant drum of many hoofs.

Ethan Scott's voice cut sharply across the hush: "Get off the streets!"

Then Scott turned to Guy Murvain. "After this hour you'll see no more of me, Murvain. That's Henry Dierkes calling on your town, my friend—and you'd be smart to go over to your own side of Bow Street."

Murvain's eyes widened and without speaking he wheeled, strode off the porch and ran west across the street.

Quick to hear and quick to understand, the crowd
faded back in both directions along Third and northward
along Bow, retreating from the swelling thunder of a score
of armed horsemen breasting the distant foot of the town.

MacIver moved then, his dripping yellow slicker swaying
loosely. Rank and steamy smells floated past him. He
crossed six feet of mud up to his ankles and rose up on the
porch with rainwater pouring from the funnel trough of his
hat in a stream before his face. He stood with his back to
the street, watching Ethan Scott's rock-hard face, and
silence grew thick between them while Scott slowly lifted
a hand and touched the points of his mustache and slowly
dropped his hand again. It was MacIver who broke the
silence: "Get out of here, you fool!"

"It has to be settled," Scott said. "Stand out of the
way, Krayle."

"No, damn it! I won't watch you die for stubbornness,
Ethan!"

"It isn't stubbornness, Krayle."

"Get out while you still can!"

Scott's lips curled back and he spat out his two words
in a harsh, crackling tone that MacIver had never heard
him use: "Get inside!"

It was the deadly light behind Scott's eyes that made
MacIver turn aside and walk past him into the deserted
saloon, almost against his will. He moved numbly; he
stepped aside from the door and turned to the nearest
window, and then for the first time saw the lonely shape
huddled there—Marla.

Her face was drawn and dismal; she didn't look at
him; her gaze was fixed on the wide back of Ethan Scott,
not twenty feet away down the porch.

MacIver's glance flicked to the opposite corner of the
intersection and he saw the first of the trotting horsemen
appear around that building and pound forward. The
others were packed in a close knot behind. He saw at least
twenty in the party. In the lead rode Henry Dierkes and a
tall man in a derby hat—and MacIver breathed, "That's
John San Saba!"

But no one was there to hear him. When he turned to

look, Marla was almost up to the door. Her pace was steady.

"No!" he shouted; he broke into a run. But she didn't hear him, or perhaps she did hear him; she walked outside and the door came back on its spring and slammed into MacIver's hand and he found himself cursing lividly, reaching under his coat for his gun.

Only it wasn't there. It was in his office, holstered on top of his safe.

"Oh, God!"

And outside, Henry Dierkes spoke just a single word: "Scott—"

Everything else Dierkes might have said was cut off by the pound of gunfire.

It was Marla who leaped in front of Scott, Marla who took the weight of the bullets while Scott's glistening guns lifted and Scott stood motionless, his feet spread a foot or so, his coattails lifting, his face as blank as a mountainside. The rattle of gunfire pounded and crashed against MacIver's soul. He hung suspended, motionless; he could not breathe. He saw Marla drop, exposing Scott; he saw the guns rock and buck against Scott's sure hands, spewing long tongues of orange flame from their muzzles, roaring out a staccato signal. A bullet nicked a slice out of MacIver's ear and his head whipped half around in reaction. He saw the derby-hatted San Saba lurch in the saddle and fall off the far side of his horse while Henry Dierkes screamed an oath, threw up his long arms and pitched away, dead on the back of a bucking horse.

Scott's guns were searching out other targets but Marla was down and Dierkes's coat whipped up and down with the bullets that struck it and finally, when the last load was fired from Scott's guns, his supreme will failed him and he sank to his knees. The big forty-fives rolled out of his limp fists and he rolled off the porch into the mud, but not before MacIver saw the dark clot above the bridge of his nose. It had taken that to kill Ethan Scott.

Victorious but leaderless, the toughs broke. Horses wheeled and collided and reared; men shouted and in whirling violence they split away and ran down Bow Street at a dead run, leaving behind them a gray and driving rain.

Dierkes and San Saba and three other men lay sprawled on the street. One man was staggering away afoot with a bullet through his leg. Scott had taken that toll. On the dry boards of the porch Marla was a crumpled shape, a darker lump of shadow among many shadows. She lifted her arm and let it drop over the side of the porch so that it touched Scott's arm; she became still.

Blood was warm and moist dripping down MacIver's neck from the bullet-slice in his ear. He lifted his hands; they were motionless and then they chattered; he touched the door and pushed.

XIV

THEY WERE four who stood on the hill, two on each side of the fresh open graves. It might have been midnight; it might have been as late as four in the morning. There was no moon, no stars, but only the thinly falling rain and the flickering light of a lantern hung on the side of the buggy. Far above to the east a faint glow marked Peacock Gorge, but none of them noticed that. MacIver touched a hand to the bandaged side of his head and looked across the wooden coffins, across the graves, at the fat, dripping face of Eugenio Castillo and at the shadowed face of Sandy, the Nugget's head bartender. "All right," MacIver said hollowly, and put his hat on before picking up his shovel and tossing the first dirt atop the boxes.

It was a lonely service, in the dead of a rainy night high on a hilltop. The work was quickly and grimly done without talk; afterward, a wooden cross lashed together with rawhide thongs served as the marker for the double grave.

He had left the bodies of Dierkes and San Saba and the toughs in the street for the town to bury; but this had been MacIver's job and now, when it was done, he looked up and watched Sandy slap his shovel atop the muddy mound and toss the shovel aside. MacIver dropped his with it. Sandy said, "He was a great man."

"He was a man," MacIver answered; Sandy dipped his head. MacIver said, "What now?"

"I'm a bartender," Sandy said. "I've got a job to do." He turned and walked away into the darkness.

Eugenio Castillo, who was no longer a peace officer, met MacIver's glance across the grave and said, "*Adios*," and walked to his waiting horse. Presently he too was absorbed by the night. MacIver looked once more at the earth mound; he thought, *Maybe she hasn't lost him*. He turned and took Nita Matlock's arm and walked downhill to the buggy. He lifted her inside and climbed up under the poor protection of the buggy and pushed his fat leather satchel under the seat, and looked at the girl sitting beside him; for MacIver did not intend to return to town. Nita said nothing. After a while MacIver said, "No one understood him."

"Did you?"

"I think so. I think I was beginning to understand. It wasn't Henry Dierkes who killed him. It was his own pride—but that's a good thing. A man's nothing without pride. He was a proud man and I feel no regret for him. He didn't care about facing them, but he had to face himself—and he did it at the last, when he knew he'd lost his edge."

"I wish," Nita said, "that I had known him."

MacIver nodded faintly; it had been a privilege. He said, "It's a funny thing—I never fired a shot through this whole thing."

"It's a good thing."

"Is it? I can't convince myself."

"That was his job, not yours."

"I might have helped him, if I'd had a gun."

"There were twenty—you couldn't have saved him."

"No," he said. "I couldn't have saved his life, but I might have saved myself."

"It was an accident. You didn't leave the gun behind on purpose."

"That's no answer to it," he said slowly; "I'll have to live with it a while, and see."

She didn't answer him, and after a while he looked past her, down the hill toward the dimly lit streets of Lodestar. He said, "Down there—they've got the peace they wanted."

"None of them will ever have peace," Nita said. "Not after tonight. This will rest on the whole town's conscience—everyone in it."

"No," MacIver said. "They'll forget. They always forget nights like this one. They have that ability, to put unpleasant things from their minds. That's how they keep themselves clean. It's how they perpetuate their own sets of pious principles. The vultures have got Lodestar."

Her face turned. "What?"

"Nothing," he said bleakly. He released the brake and lifted the reins and clucked to the horse.

ABOUT THE AUTHOR

Born in 1939, Brian Garfield began writing short stories at
age twelve and wrote his first published novel when he
was 18 (*Range Justice*, 1960). Having grown up on South-
western ranches, he turned his literary talents to the
American West and immediately established a reputation
as one of the finest Western novelists of his generation.

He found time to graduate from the University of
Arizona (B.A., 1959) and complete his graduate studies
(M.A., 1963), to teach, to tour with a professional jazz
band, and to serve in the U.S. Army and Army Reserve
(1957-65). Since 1963 he has been a fulltime writer of
novels, short stories, and screenplays.

Garfield has produced nearly seventy books of fiction
and nonfiction, including *Death Wish*, *Hopscotch* (winner
of the Edgar Award and basis for the popular film), *The
Paladin*, *Wild Times* (nominated for the American Book
Award and filmed as a TV miniseries), *The Thousand-Mile
War*, *Western Films*, *Kolchak's Gold*, *Relentless*, and *Tripwire*.
As president of his own film company, Garfield has over-
seen production of two of his own properties. He is also
the only person ever to have served as president of both
the Mystery Writers of America and the Western Writers
of America.

In short, this prolific author is very difficult to type-
cast. Always writing, Garfield is a frequent traveler, col-
lege lecturer, and guest on radio and television interview
shows. With over 17 million copies of his books sold
worldwide (in eighteen languages), Brian Garfield is currently
at work on a major historical novel. He and his wife Bina
live in Southern California.

Roe Richmond is one of that rare breed of Western writers whose novels continue to be read by generation after generation. In the tradition of Luke Short and Ernest Haycox, he is a storyteller of power and passion who brings back to life the authentic Old West.

Roe Richmond has these great westerns to offer you:

There was only one man who had the guts, the guns and the driving, urgent reason to buck that crew of rustlers robbing and murdering their way through the desert: Jim Lacy, alias Texas Jack, alias "Nevada."

Bantam is proud to publish the 60th Anniversary Edition of

ZANE GREY'S
"NEVADA"

Bantam has some of the best westerns available. Check to see if some of them aren't missing from your bookshelf.

TERRY C. JOHNSTON

Winner of the prestigious Western Writer's award for best first novel, Terry C. Johnston brings you two volumes of his award-winning saga of mountain men Josiah Paddock and Titus Bass who strive together to meet the challenges of the western wilderness in the 1830's.

☐ 25572 **CARRY THE WIND** $4.95

Having killed a wealthy young Frenchman in a duel, Josiah Paddock flees St. Louis in 1831. He heads west to the fierce and beautiful Rocky Mountains, to become a free trapper far from the entanglements of civilization. Hot-headed and impetuous, young Josiah finds his romantic image of life in the mountains giving way to a harsh struggle for survival—against wild animals, fierce Indians, and nature's own cruelty. Half-dead of cold and starvation, he encounters Titus Bass, a solitary old trapper who takes the youth under his wing and teaches him the ways of the mountains. So begins a magnificent historical novel, remarkable for its wealth of authentic mountain lore and wisdom.

☐ 26224 **BORDERLORDS** $4.95

Here is a swirling, powerful drama of the early American wilderness, filled with fascinating scenes of tribal Indian life depicted with passion and detail unequaled in American literature, and all of it leading up to a terrifying climax at the fabled 1833 Green River Rendezvous.

Look for these books wherever Bantam books are sold, or use this handy coupon for ordering:

BANTAM
SHOP·AT·HOME
C·A·T·A·L·O·G

Special Offer
Buy a Bantam Book
for only 50¢.

Now you can have Bantam's catalog filled with hundreds of titles plus take advantage of our unique and exciting bonus book offer. A special offer which gives you the opportunity to purchase a Bantam book for only 50¢. Here's how!

By ordering any five books at the regular price per order, you can also choose any other single book listed (up to a $4.95 value) for just 50¢. Some restrictions do apply, but for further details why not send for Bantam's catalog of titles today!

Just send us your name and address and we will send you a catalog!